This book is donated

in memory of

George S. Josephs

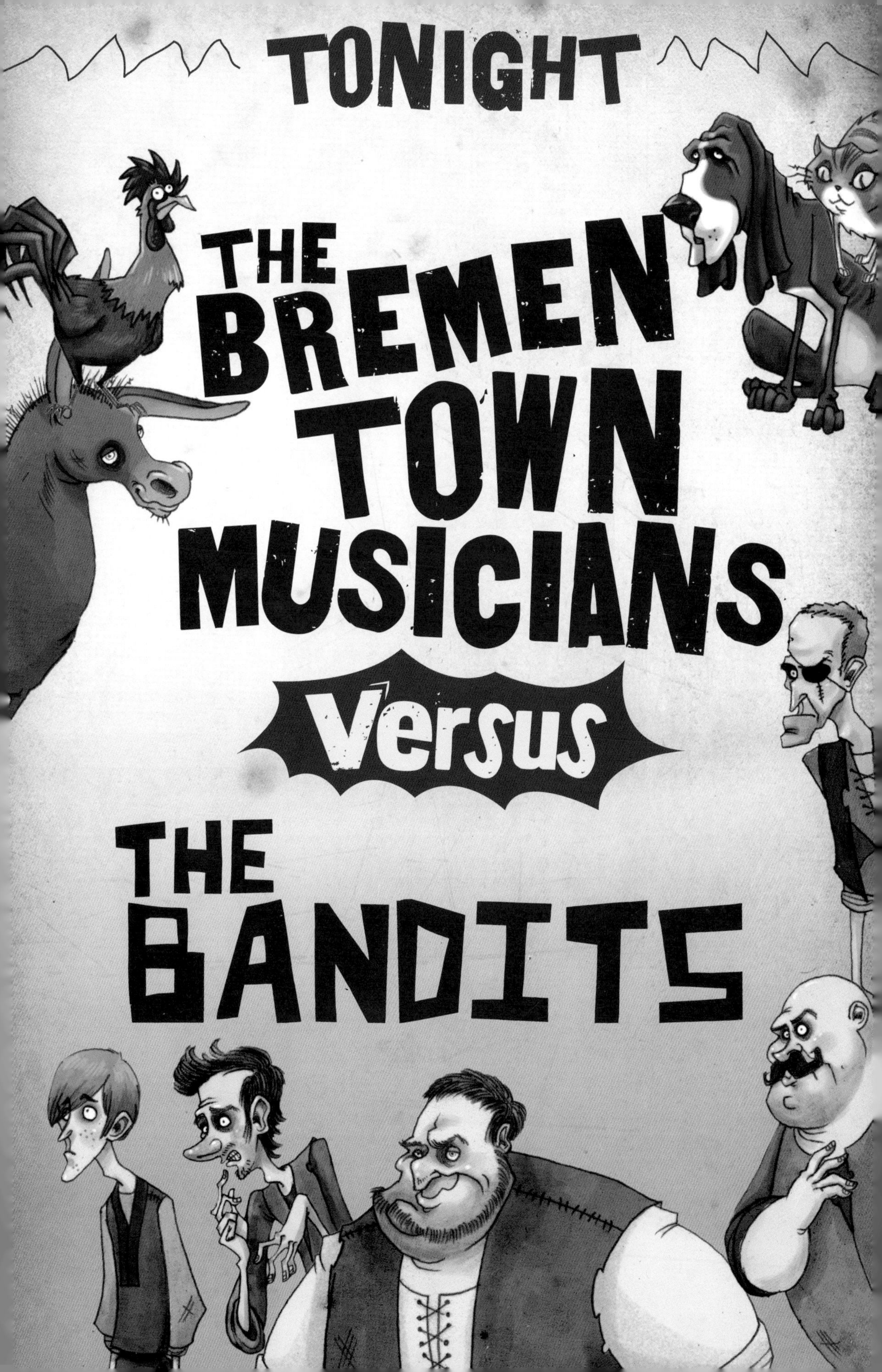
TONIGHT
THE BREMEN TOWN MUSICIANS
Versus
THE BANDITS

Graphic Spin is published by Stone Arch Books
A Capstone Imprint
151 Good Counsel Drive, P.O. Box 669
Mankato, Minnesota 56002
www.capstonepub.com

Library of Congress Cataloging-in-Publication Data
Simonson, Louise.
The Bremen town musicians : a Grimm graphic novel / written by Louise Simonson ; illustrated by Lisa K. Weber.
p. cm. -- (Graphic spin)
ISBN 978-1-4342-2518-4 (library binding)
1. Graphic novels. [1. Graphic novels. 2. Fairy tales. 3. Folklore--Germany.] I. Grimm, Jacob, 1785-1863. II. Grimm, Wilhelm, 1786-1859. III. Weber, Lisa K., ill. IV. Bremen town musicians. English. V. Title.
PZ7.7.S546Br 2011
741.5'973--dc22
2010025196

Art Director/Graphic Designer: Kay Fraser
Summary: A cranky, clever donkey. A grumpy, chubby cat. An old, loyal hound dog. A kooky, eager rooster. What do these four animals have in common? They can sing! Well, kind of. The quartet of yowling outcasts takes their musical troupe on the road to Bremen Town, but along the way, they spot some robbers counting their ill-gotten treasures in an abandoned house. Hungry and tired, the creatures hatch a plan to upend the crooked criminals — but they'll have to lean on each other to get the job done.

Printed in the United States of America in North Mankato, Minnesota.
092010
005933CGS11

A GRIMM GRAPHIC NOVEL

THE BREMEN TOWN MUSICIANS

retold by Louise Simonson

illustrated by Lisa Weber

STONE ARCH BOOKS
a capstone imprint

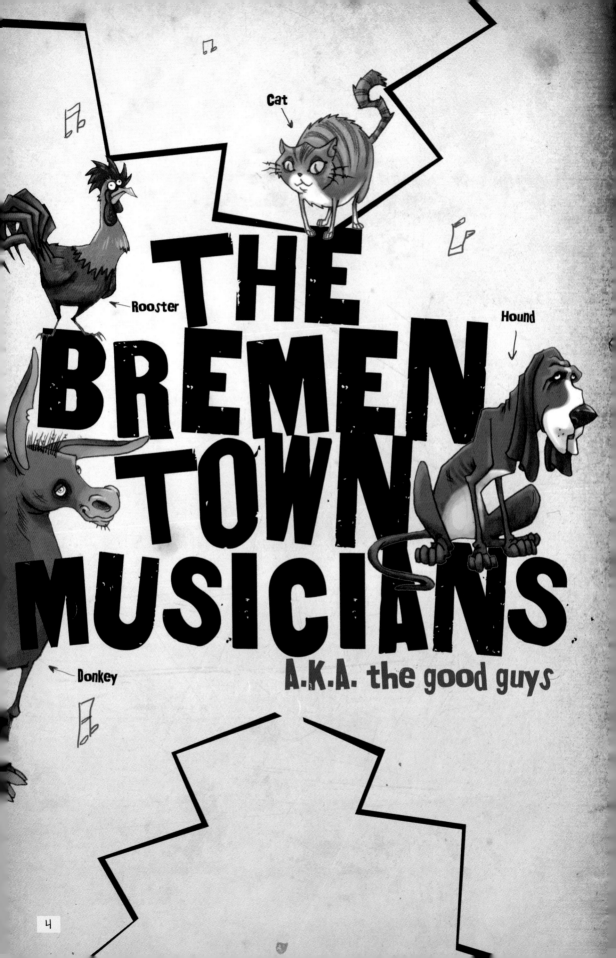

Cat

Rooster

THE BREMEN TOWN MUSICIANS

A.K.A. the good guys

Hound

Donkey

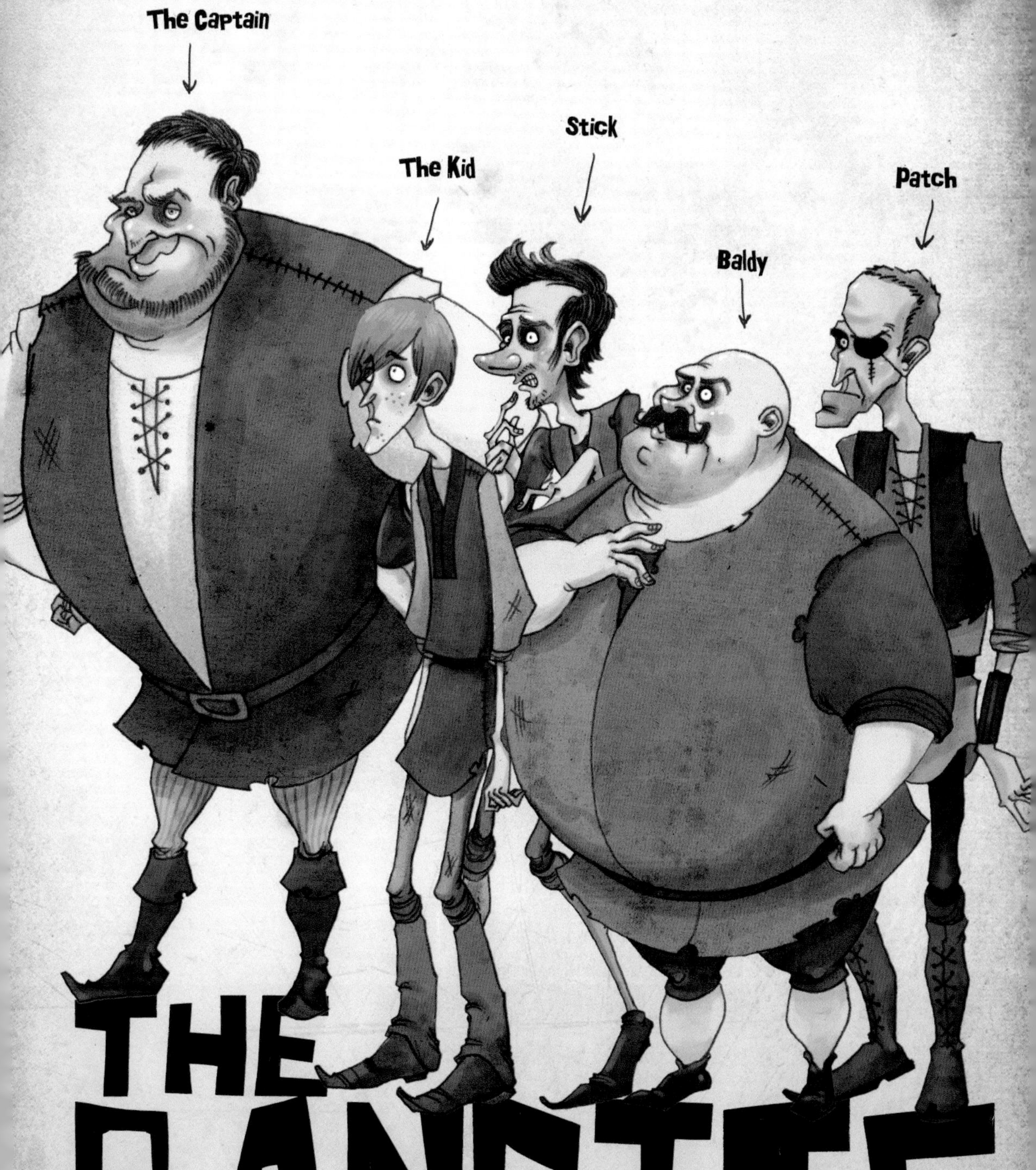
The Captain
The Kid
Stick
Baldy
Patch

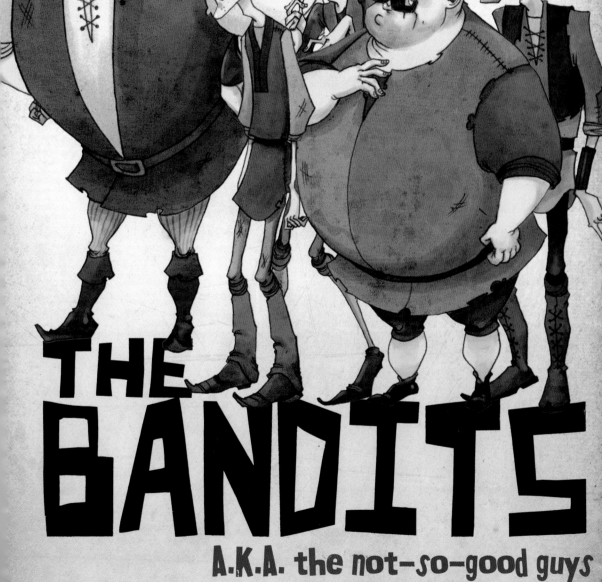

THE BANDITS

A.K.A. the not-so-good guys

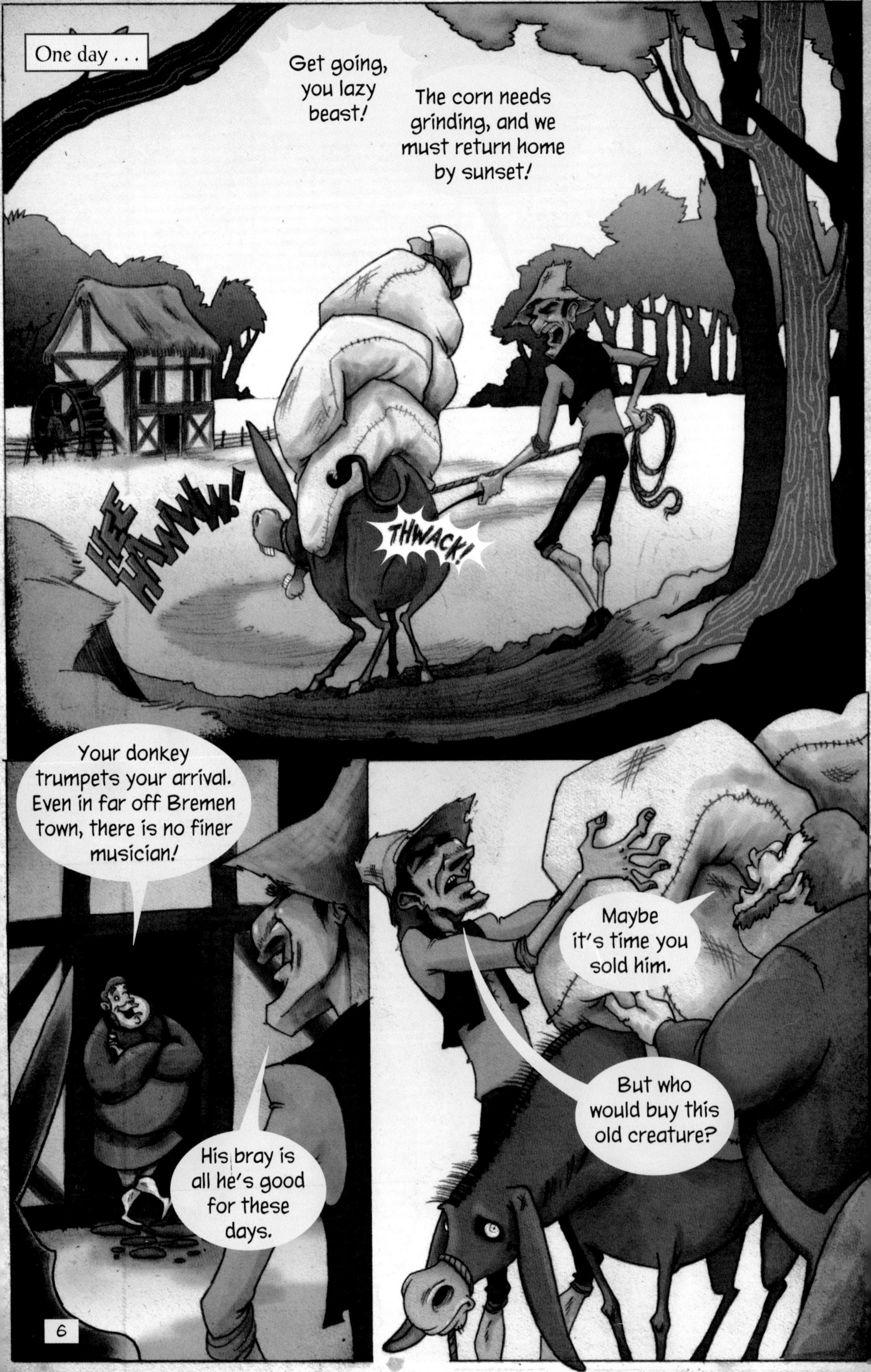
One day . . .
Get going, you lazy beast!
The corn needs grinding, and we must return home by sunset!
HEE-HAWWW!
THWACK!
Your donkey trumpets your arrival. Even in far off Bremen town, there is no finer musician!
His bray is all he's good for these days.
Maybe it's time you sold him.
But who would buy this old creature?

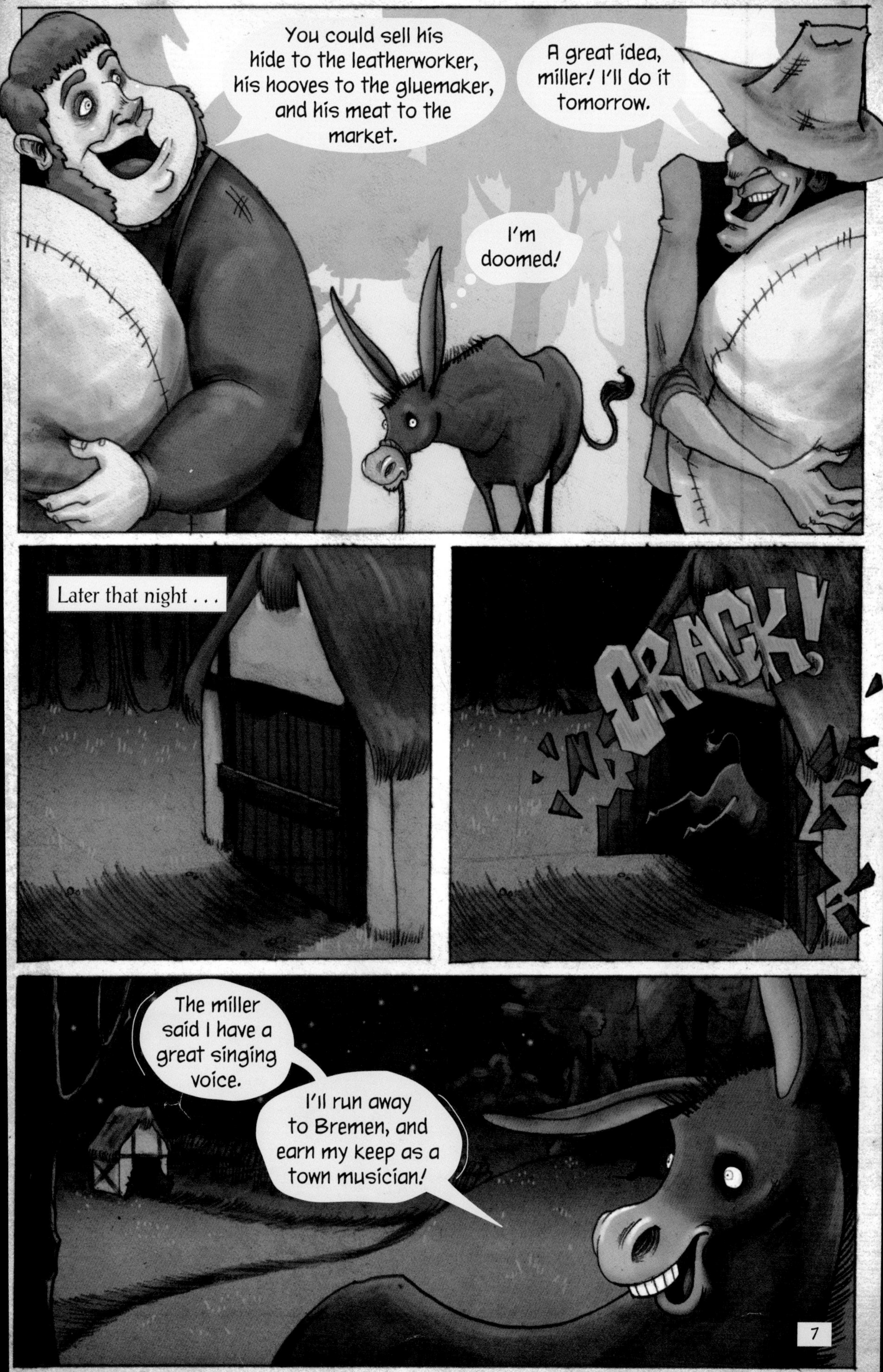
You could sell his hide to the leatherworker, his hooves to the gluemaker, and his meat to the market.
A great idea, miller! I'll do it tomorrow.
I'm doomed!
Later that night . . .
CRACK!
The miller said I have a great singing voice.
I'll run away to Bremen, and earn my keep as a town musician!

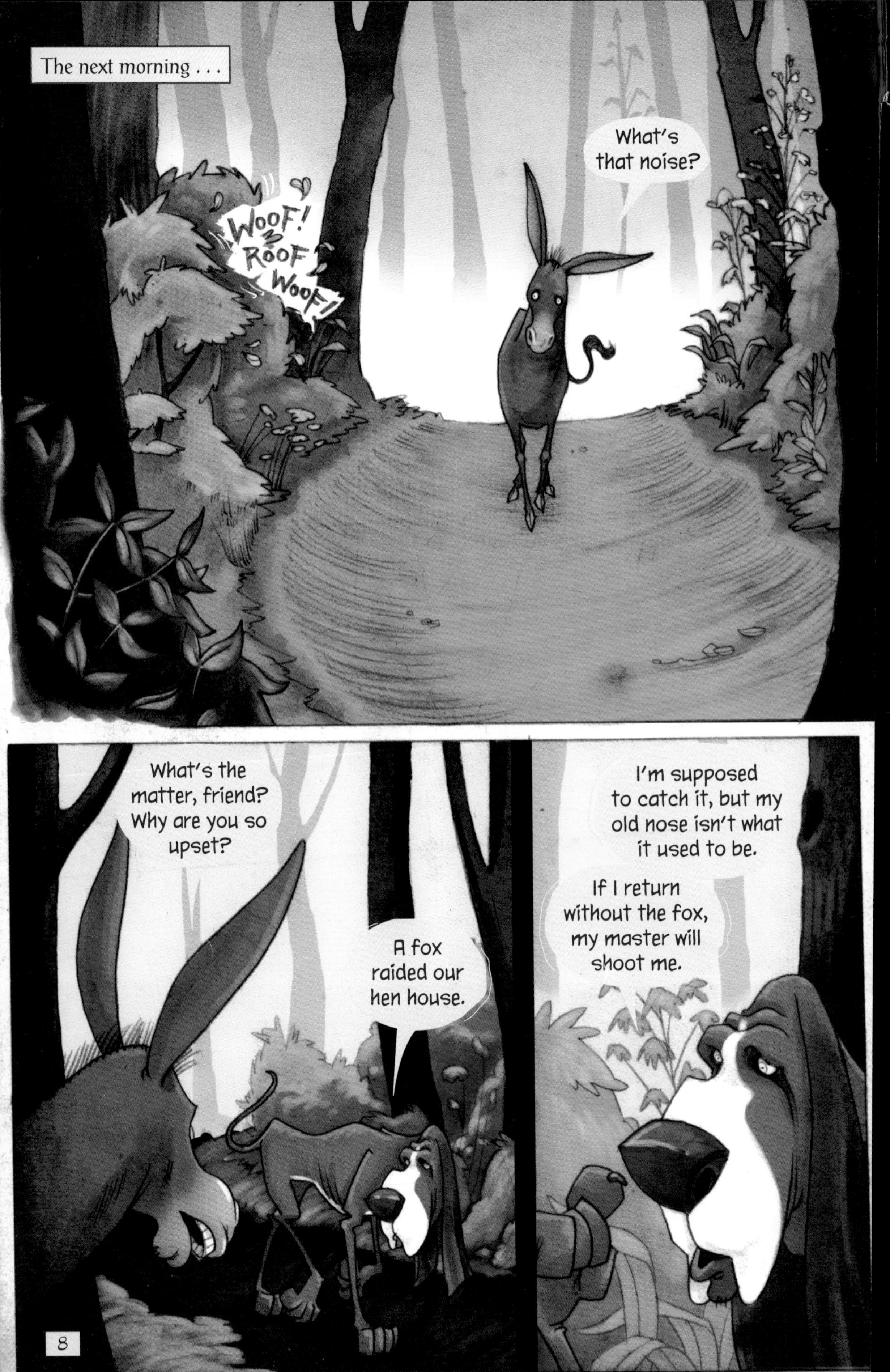

The next morning . . .
WOOF! ROOF WOOF!
What's that noise?
What's the matter, friend? Why are you so upset?
A fox raided our hen house.
I'm supposed to catch it, but my old nose isn't what it used to be.
If I return without the fox, my master will shoot me.

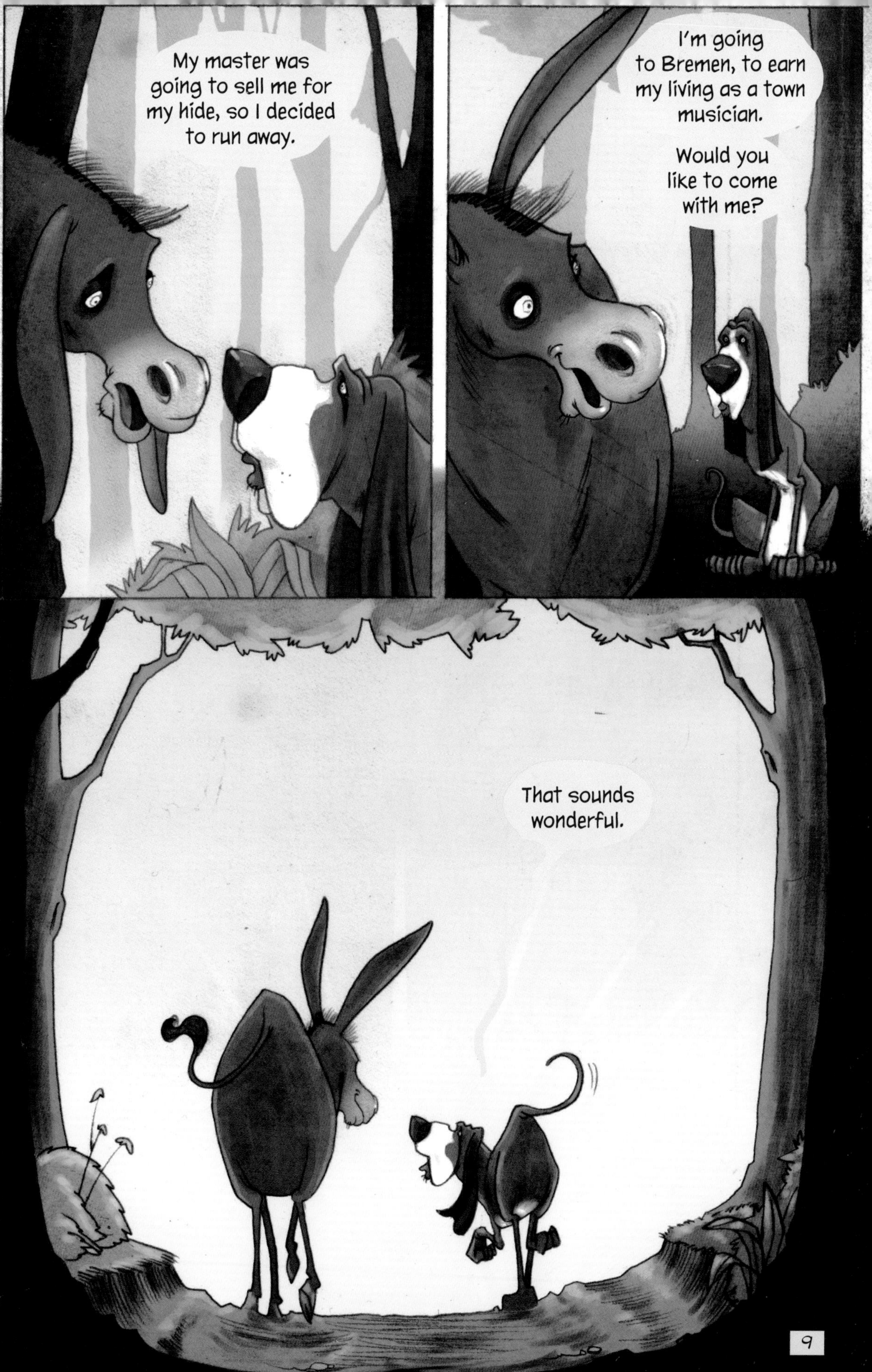
My master was going to sell me for my hide, so I decided to run away.
I'm going to Bremen, to earn my living as a town musician.
Would you like to come with me?
That sounds wonderful.

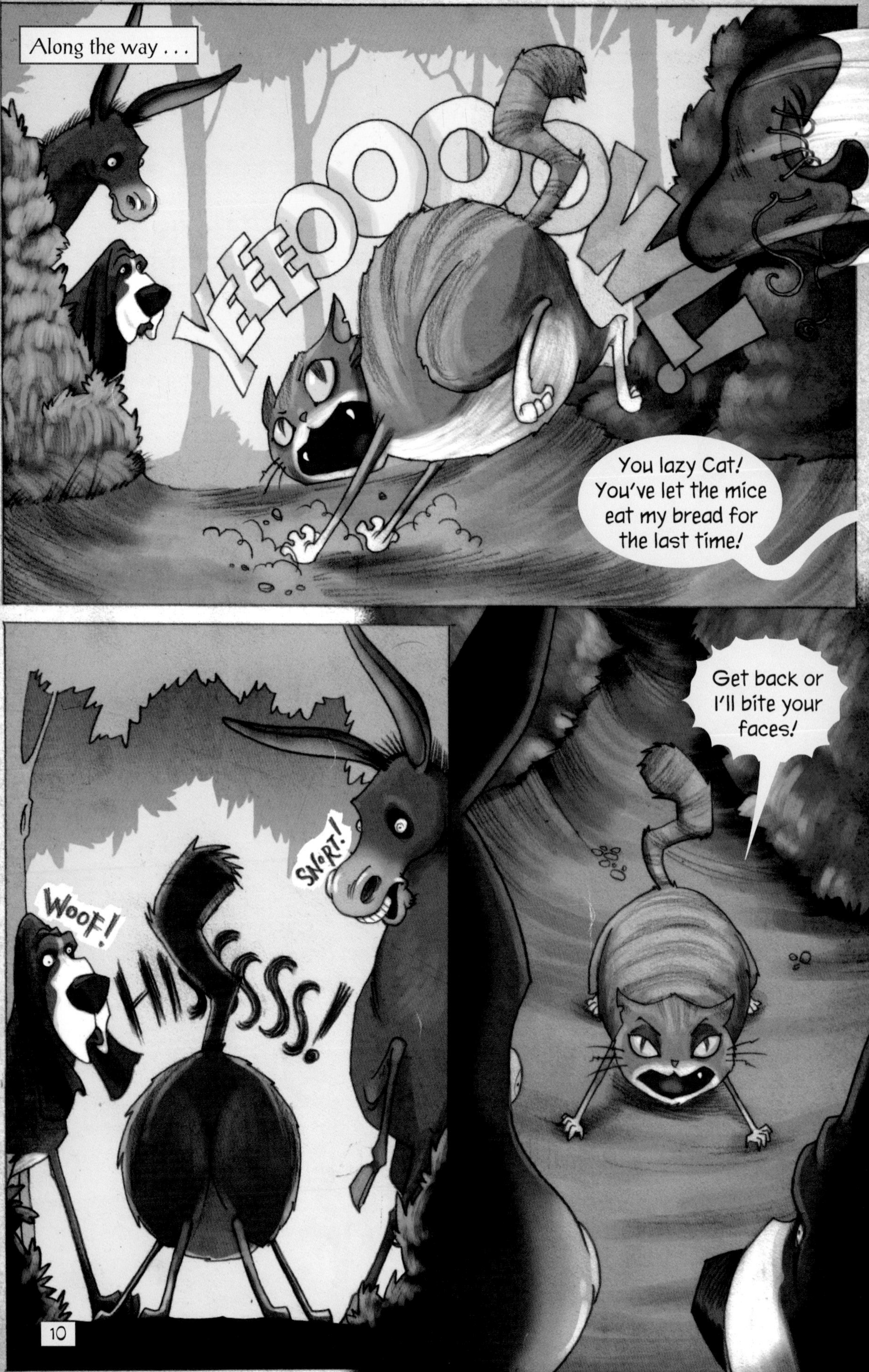

Along the way . . .
YEEOOOOOWL!
You lazy Cat! You've let the mice eat my bread for the last time!
SNORT!
WOOF!
HISSSS!
Get back or I'll bite your faces!

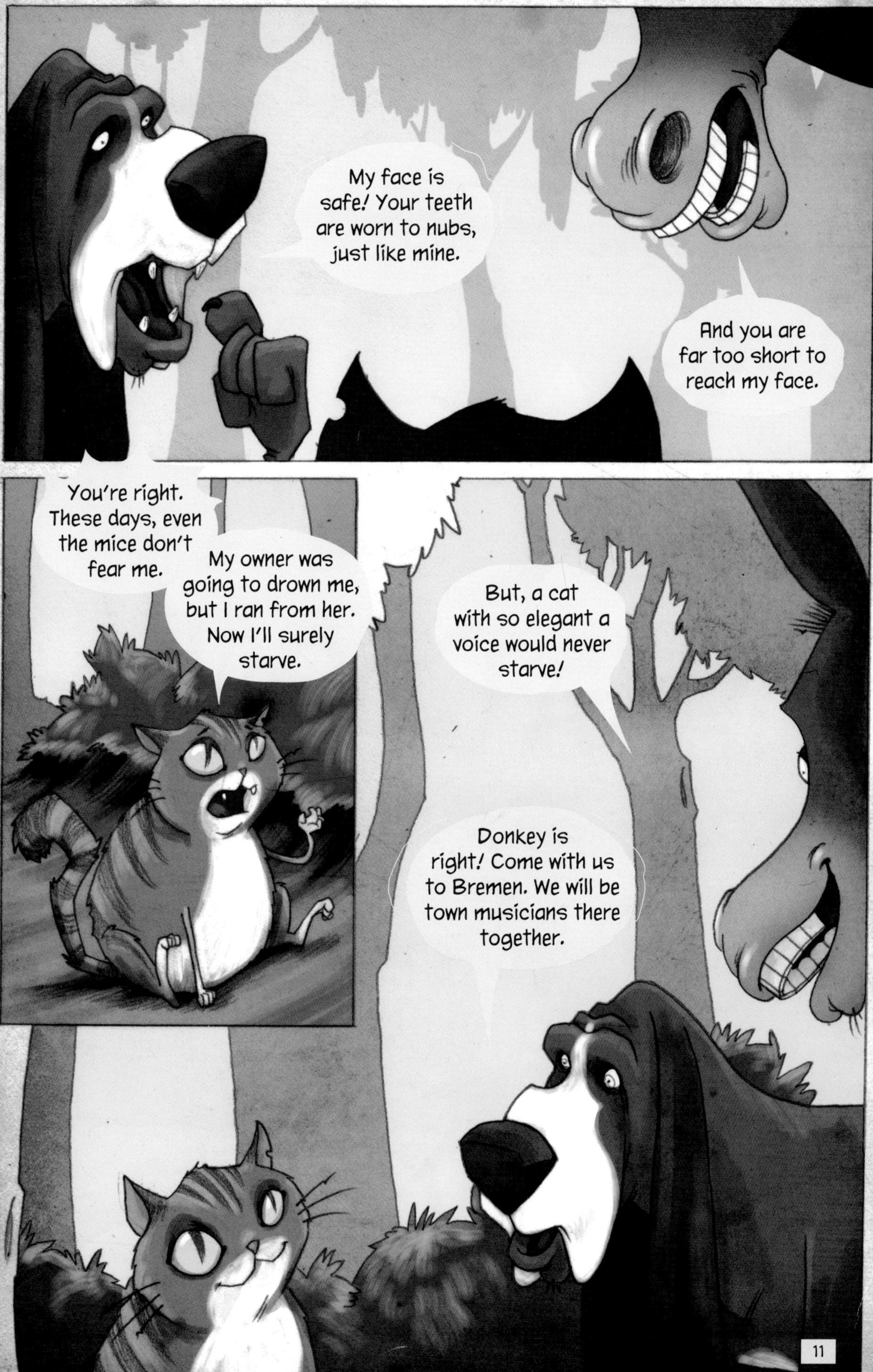
My face is safe! Your teeth are worn to nubs, just like mine.
And you are far too short to reach my face.
You're right. These days, even the mice don't fear me.
My owner was going to drown me, but I ran from her. Now I'll surely starve.
But, a cat with so elegant a voice would never starve!
Donkey is right! Come with us to Bremen. We will be town musicians there together.

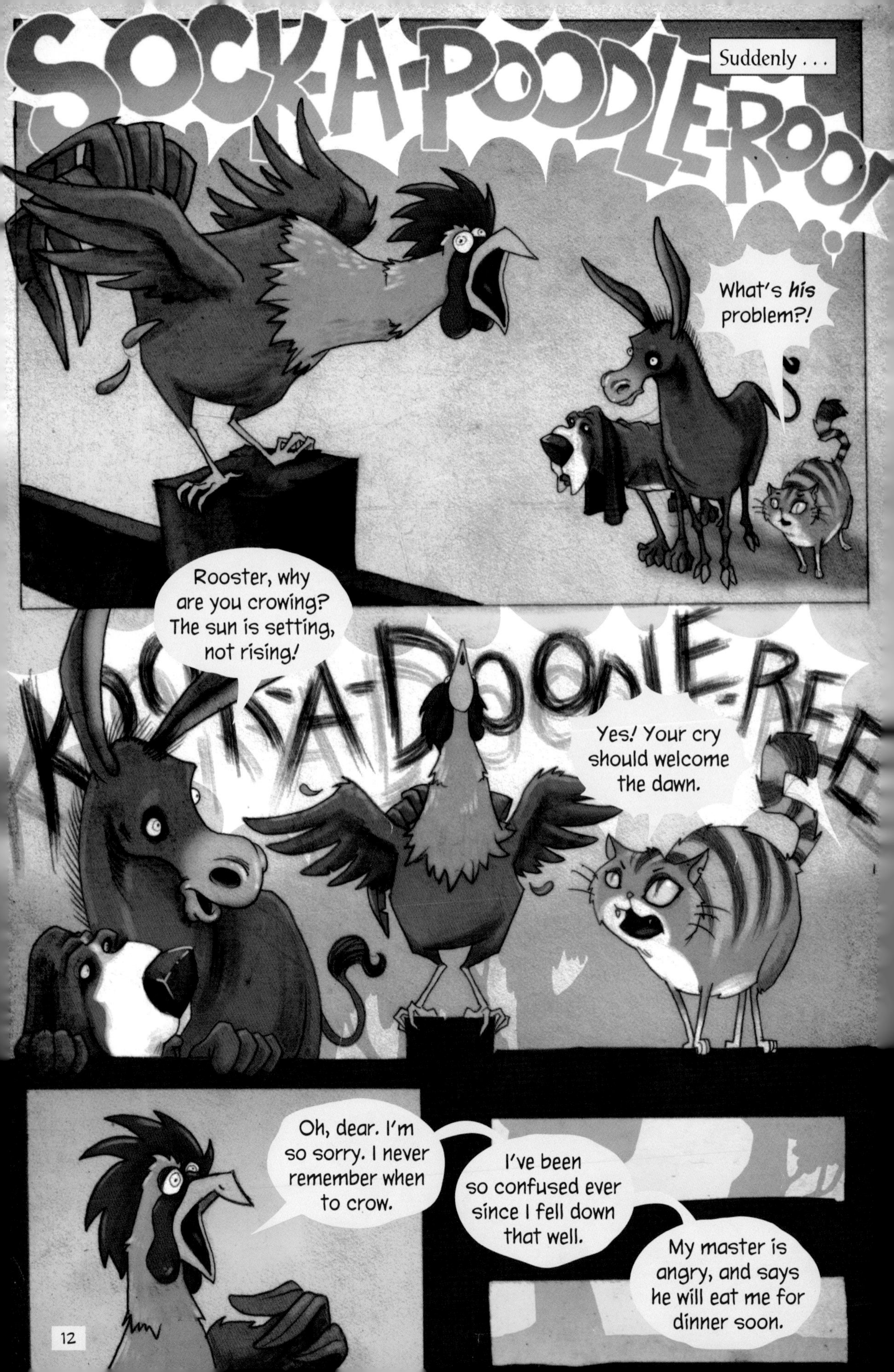
SOCK-A-POODLE-ROO!
Suddenly . . .
What's *his* problem?!
Rooster, why are you crowing? The sun is setting, not rising!
Yes! Your cry should welcome the dawn.
Oh, dear. I'm so sorry. I never remember when to crow.
I've been so confused ever since I fell down that well.
My master is angry, and says he will eat me for dinner soon.

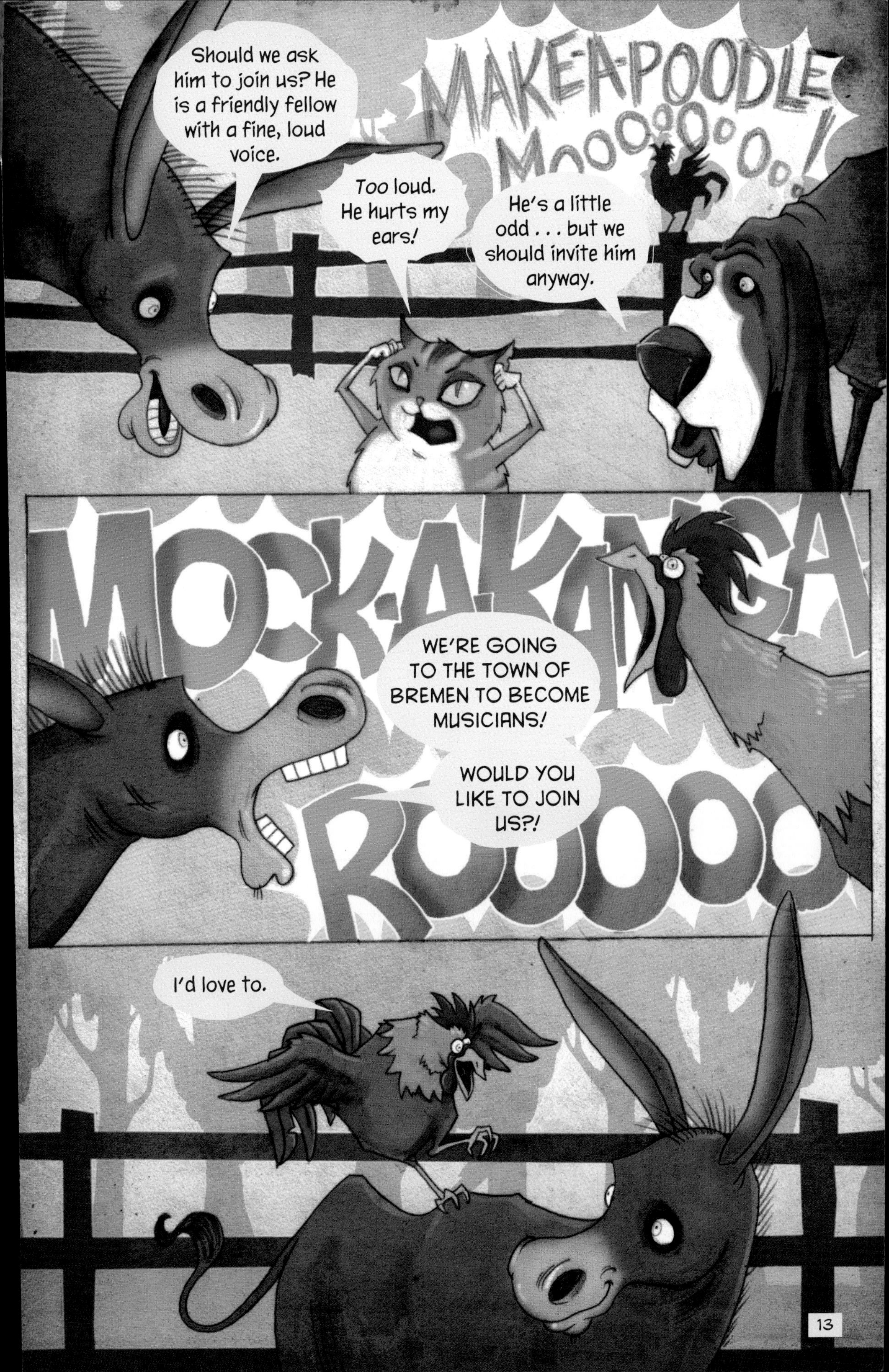

Should we ask him to join us? He is a friendly fellow with a fine, loud voice.
Too loud. He hurts my ears!
He's a little odd . . . but we should invite him anyway.
MAKE-A-POODLE MOOOOOOO!
MOCK-A-KANGA ROOOOO
WE'RE GOING TO THE TOWN OF BREMEN TO BECOME MUSICIANS!
WOULD YOU LIKE TO JOIN US?!
I'd love to.

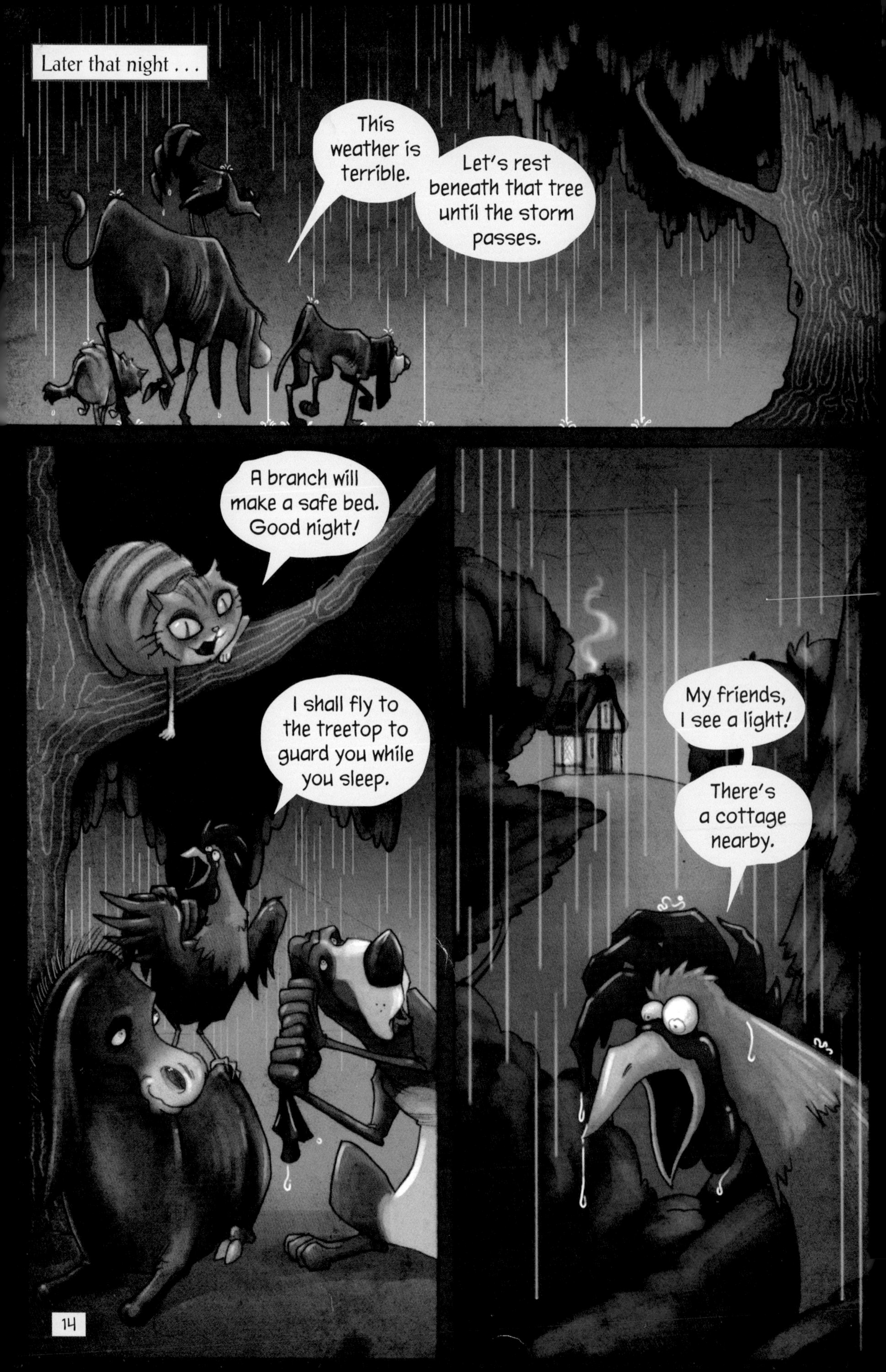
Later that night . . .
This weather is terrible.
Let's rest beneath that tree until the storm passes.
A branch will make a safe bed. Good night!
I shall fly to the treetop to guard you while you sleep.
My friends, I see a light!
There's a cottage nearby.

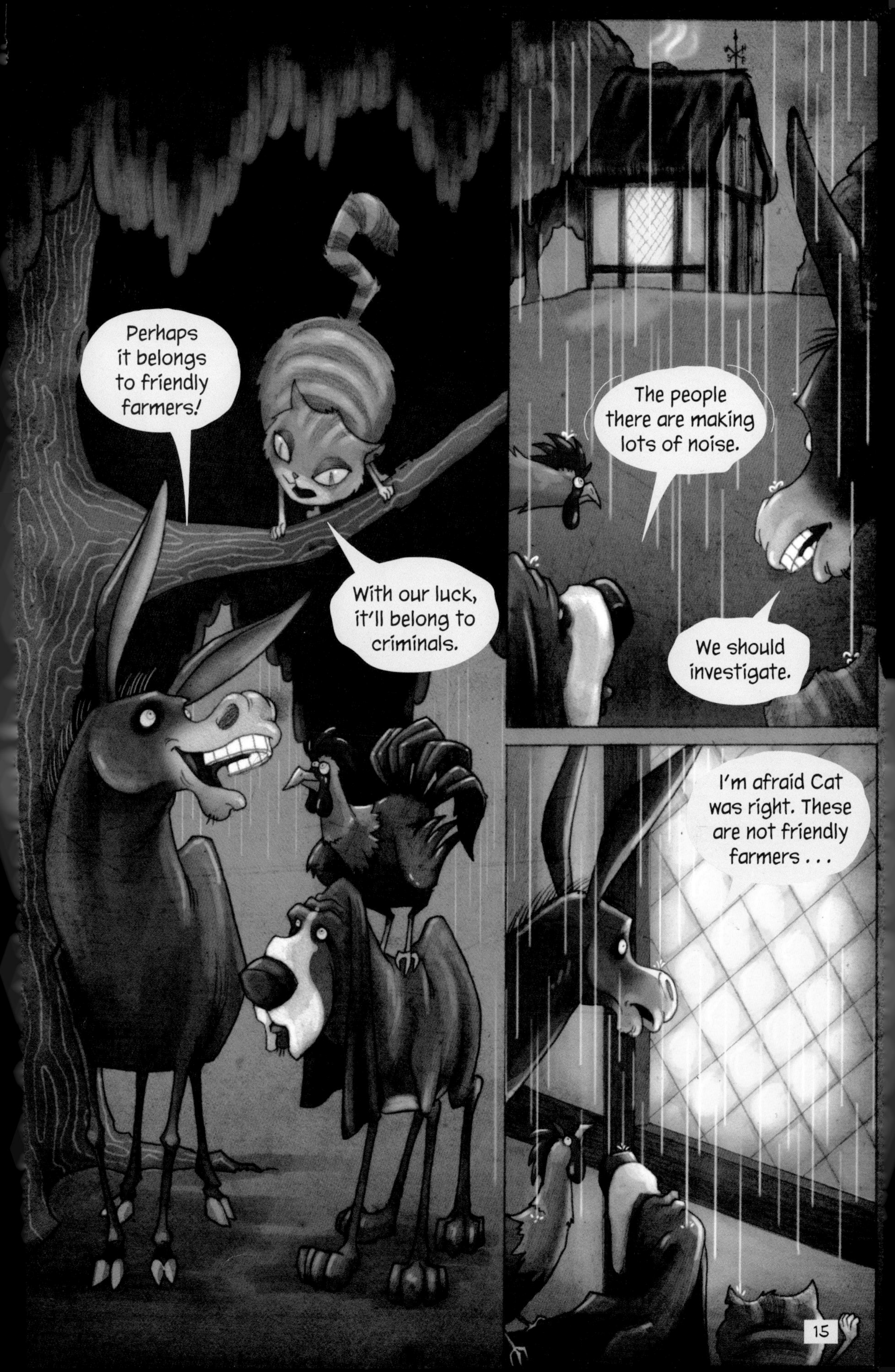
Perhaps it belongs to friendly farmers!
With our luck, it'll belong to criminals.
The people there are making lots of noise.
We should investigate.
I'm afraid Cat was right. These are not friendly farmers . . .

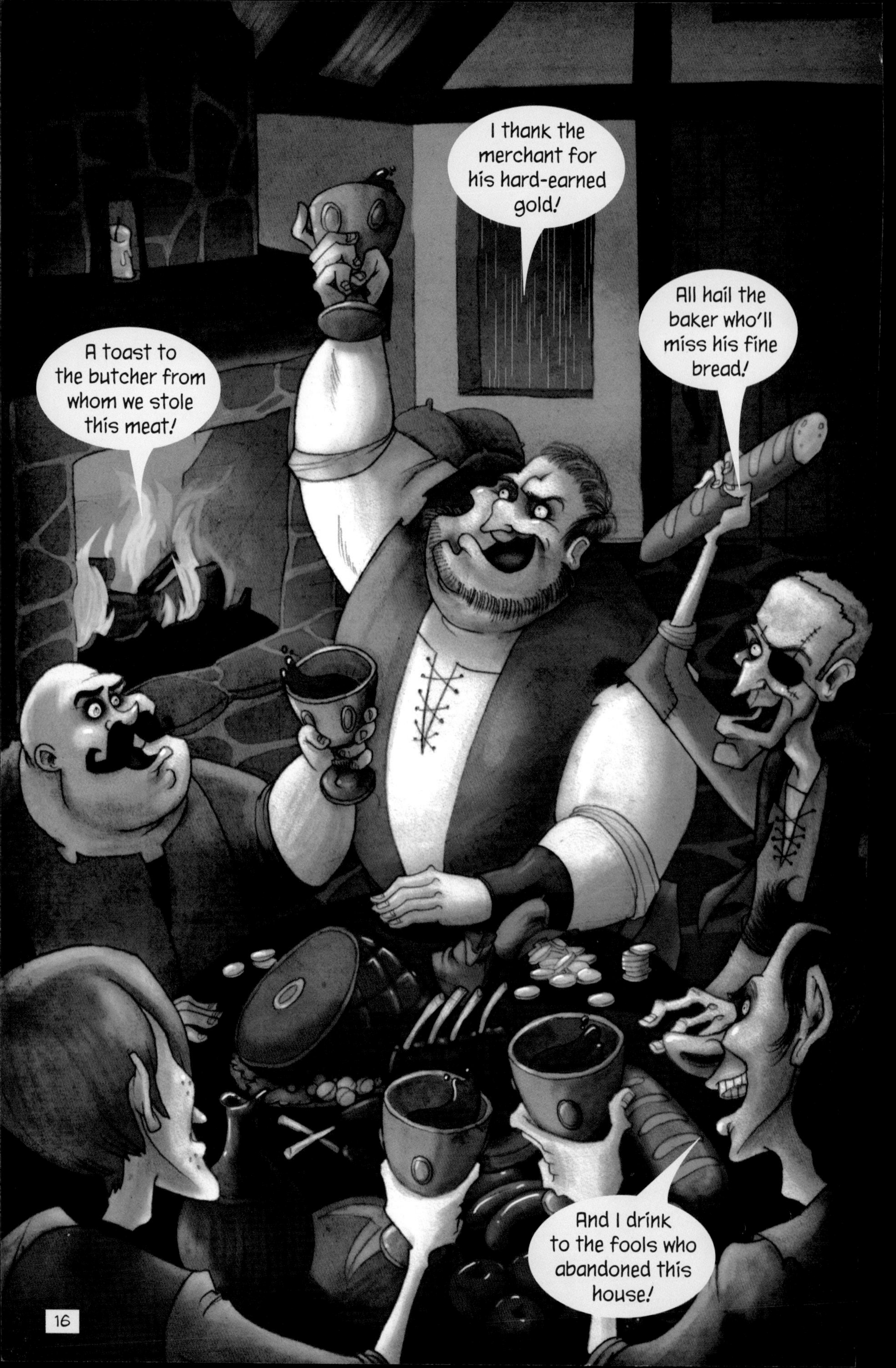
A toast to the butcher from whom we stole this meat!
I thank the merchant for his hard-earned gold!
All hail the baker who'll miss his fine bread!
And I drink to the fools who abandoned this house!

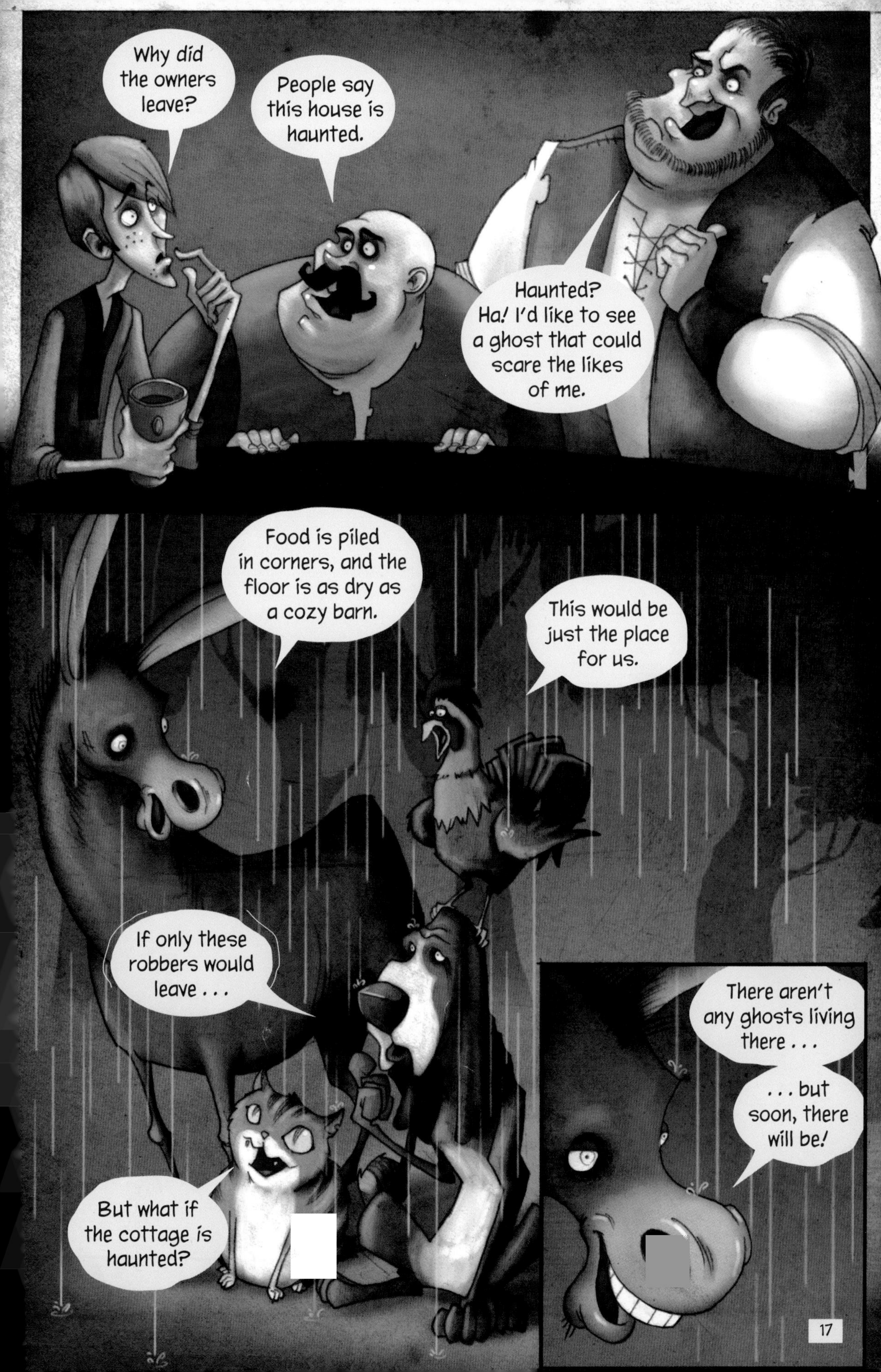
Why did the owners leave?
People say this house is haunted.
Haunted? Ha! I'd like to see a ghost that could scare the likes of me.
Food is piled in corners, and the floor is as dry as a cozy barn.
This would be just the place for us.
If only these robbers would leave . . .
But what if the cottage is haunted?
There aren't any ghosts living there . . .
. . . but soon, there will be!

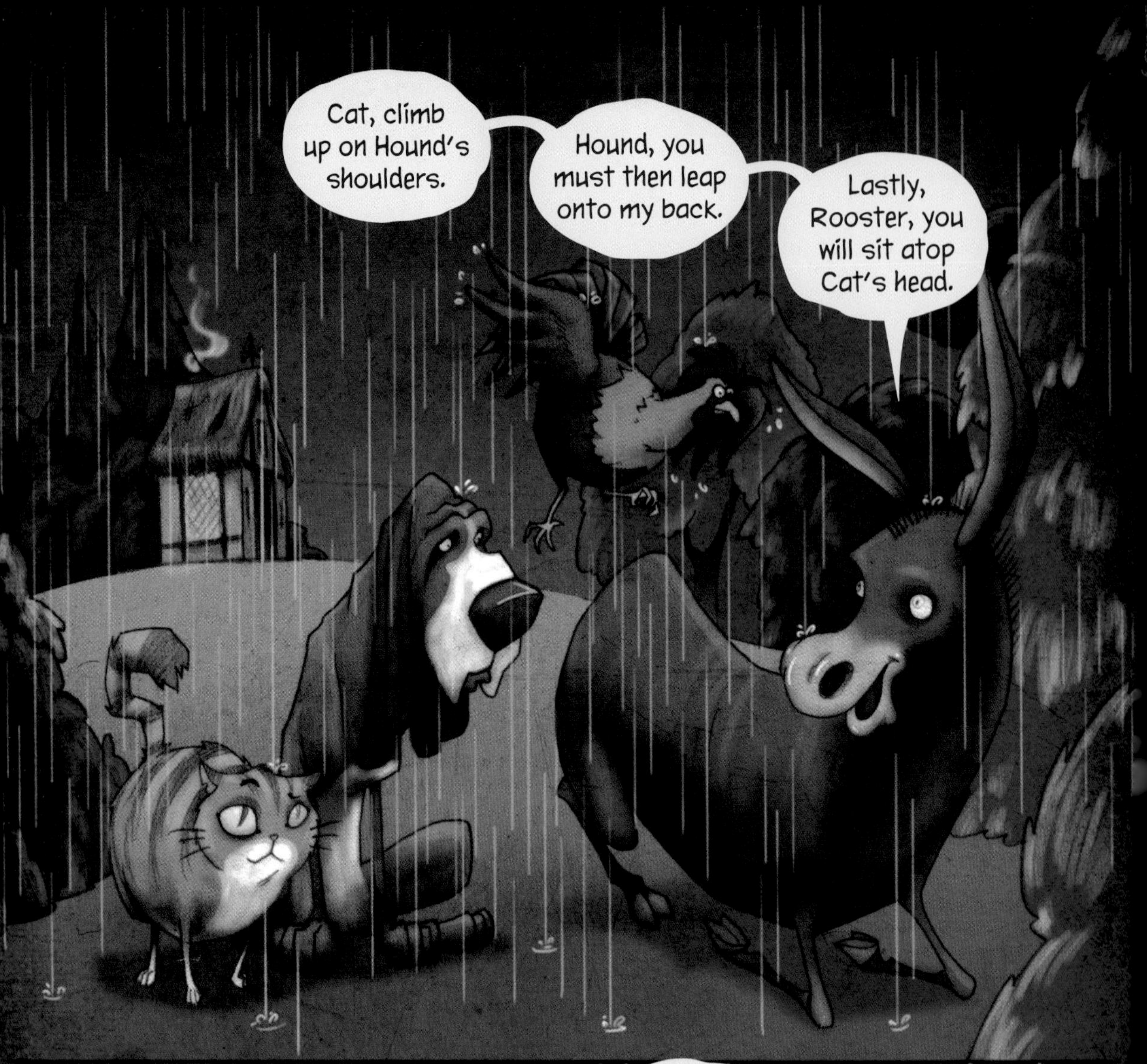
Cat, climb up on Hound's shoulders.
Hound, you must then leap onto my back.
Lastly, Rooster, you will sit atop Cat's head.
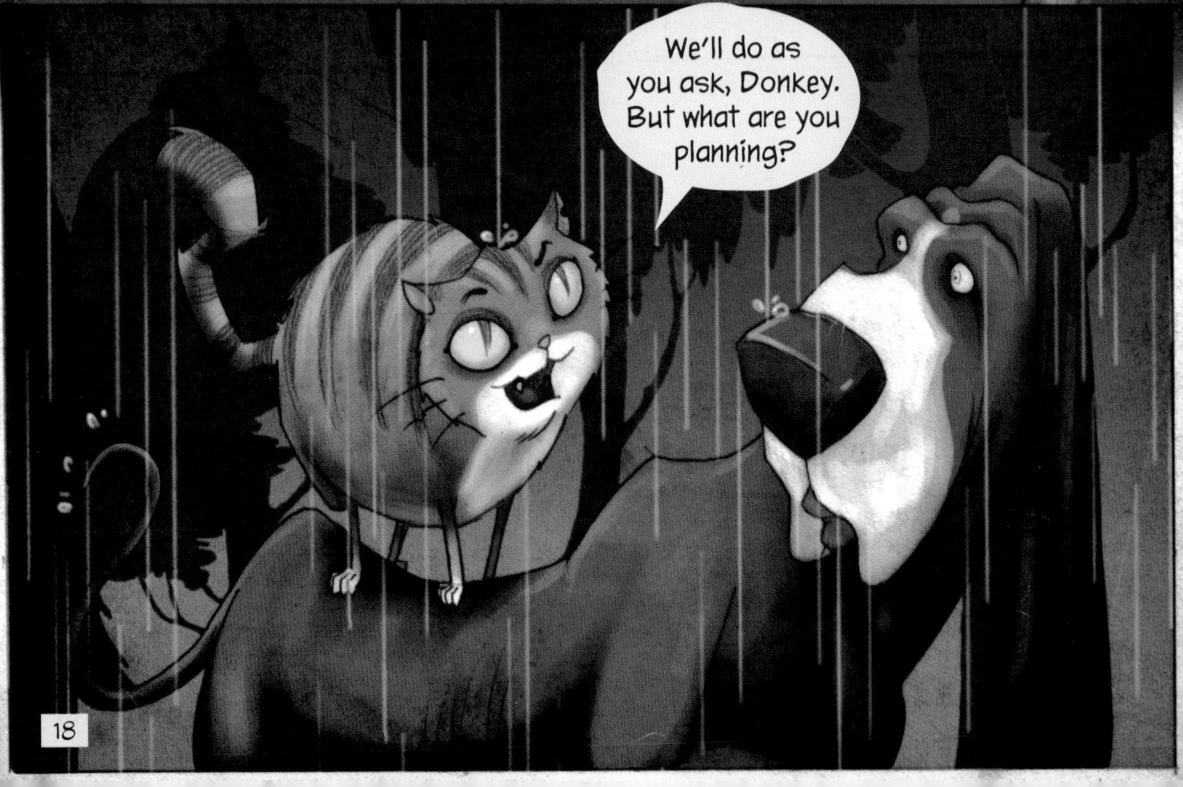
We'll do as you ask, Donkey. But what are you planning?

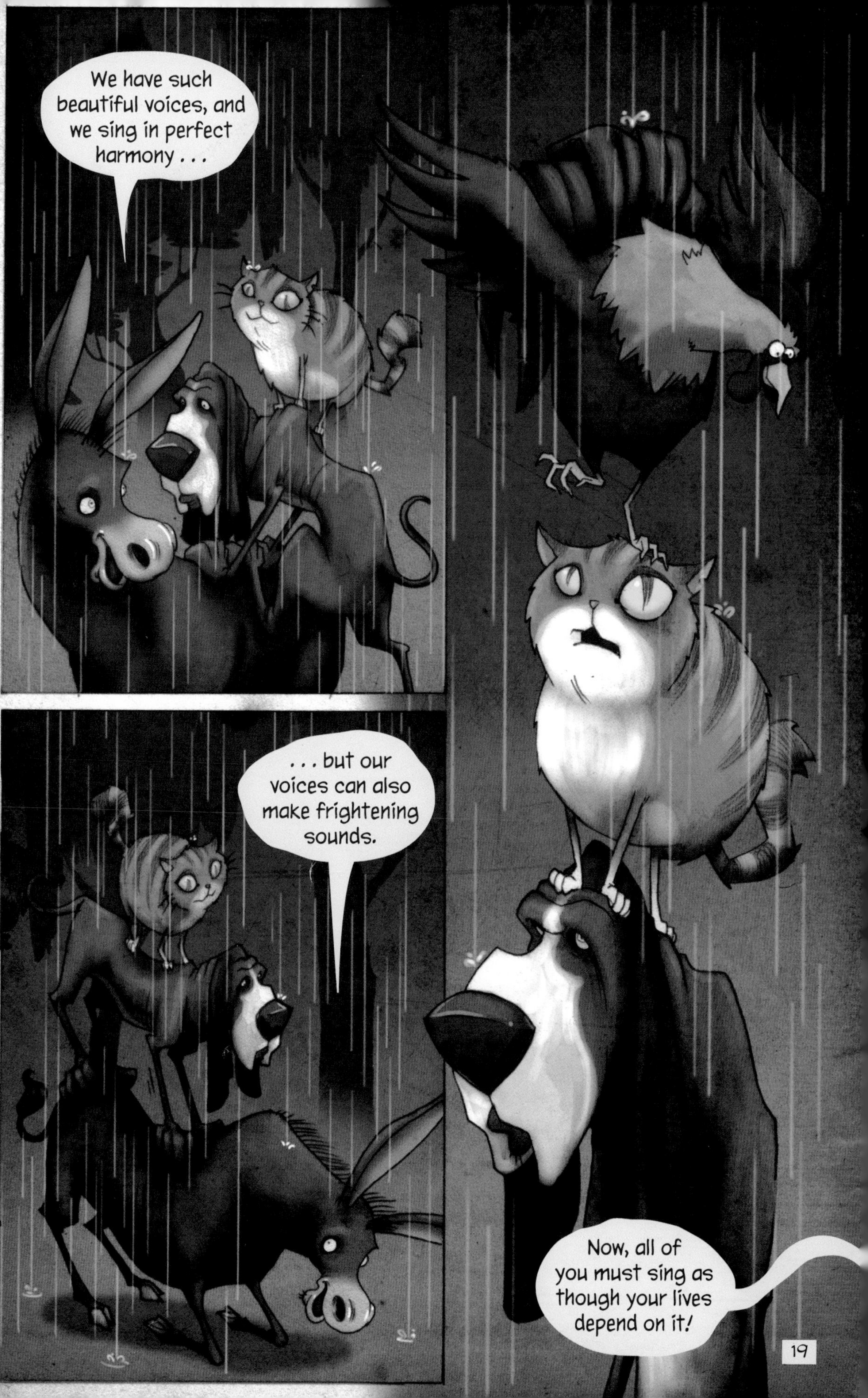
We have such beautiful voices, and we sing in perfect harmony . . .
. . . but our voices can also make frightening sounds.
Now, all of you must sing as though your lives depend on it!

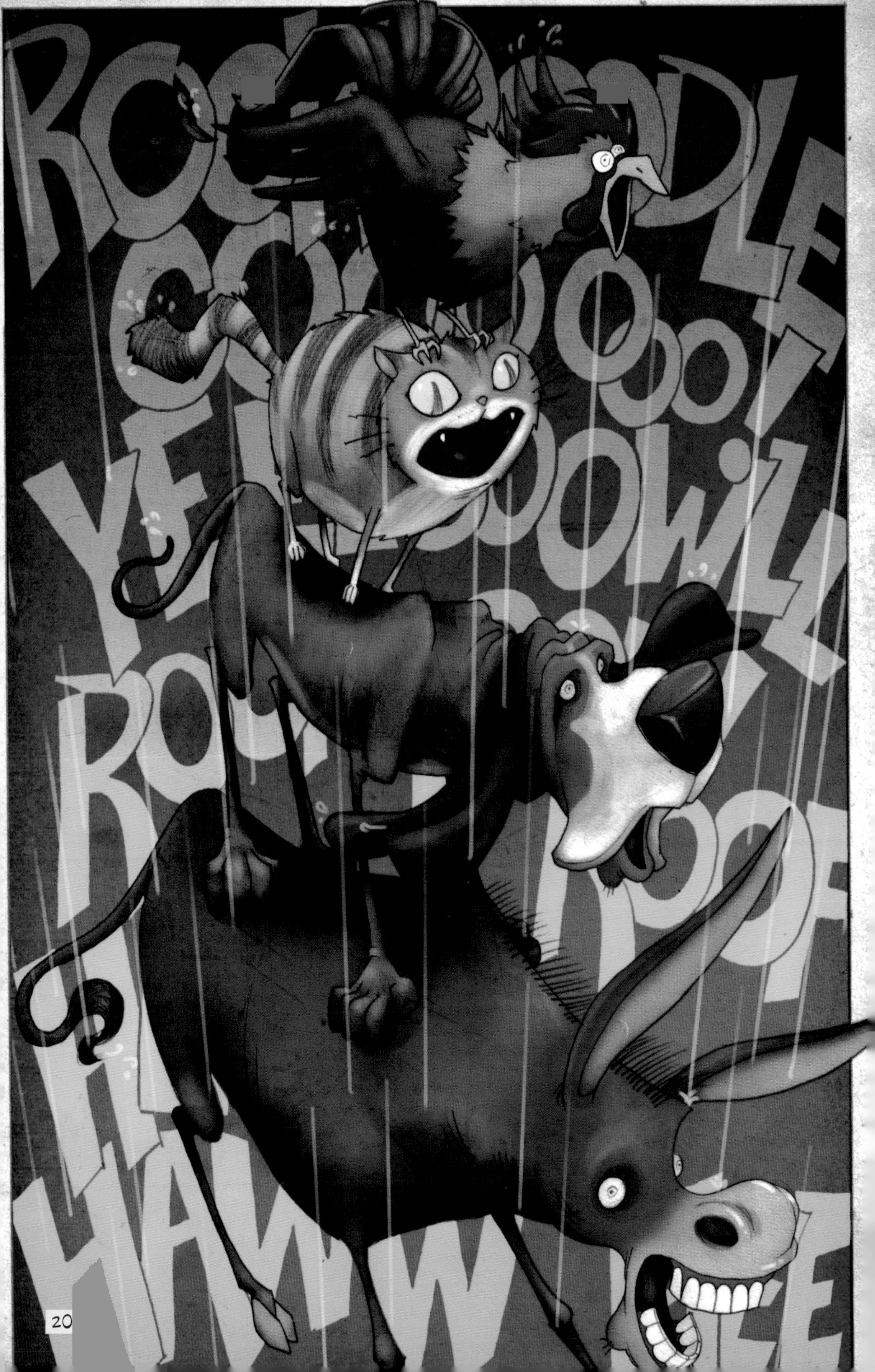

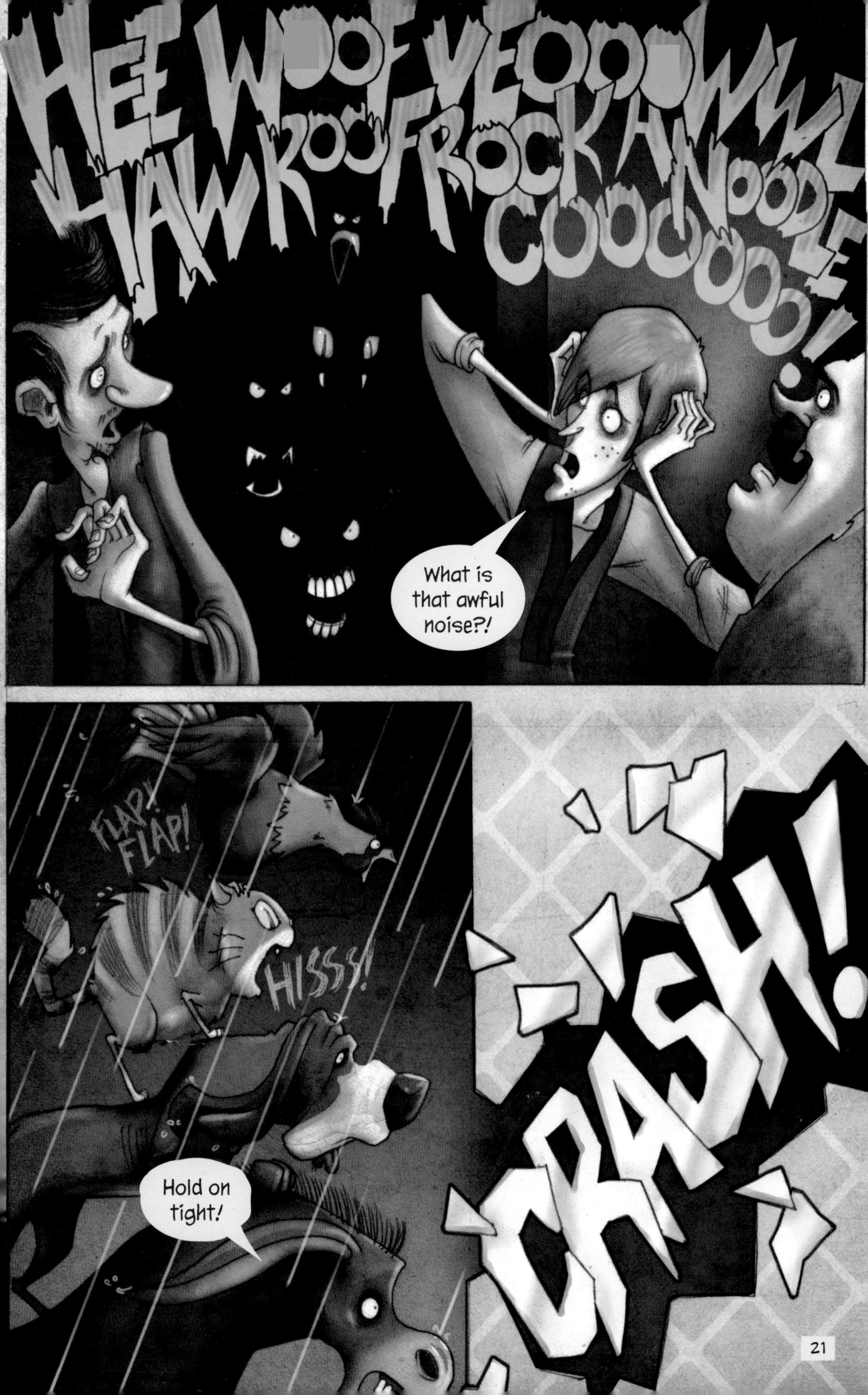
HEE WOOF VEOOOWWL
HAW ROOF ROCK A NOODLE
COOOCOOOOLE!!
What is that awful noise?!
FLAP! FLAP!
HISSS!
CRASH!
Hold on tight!

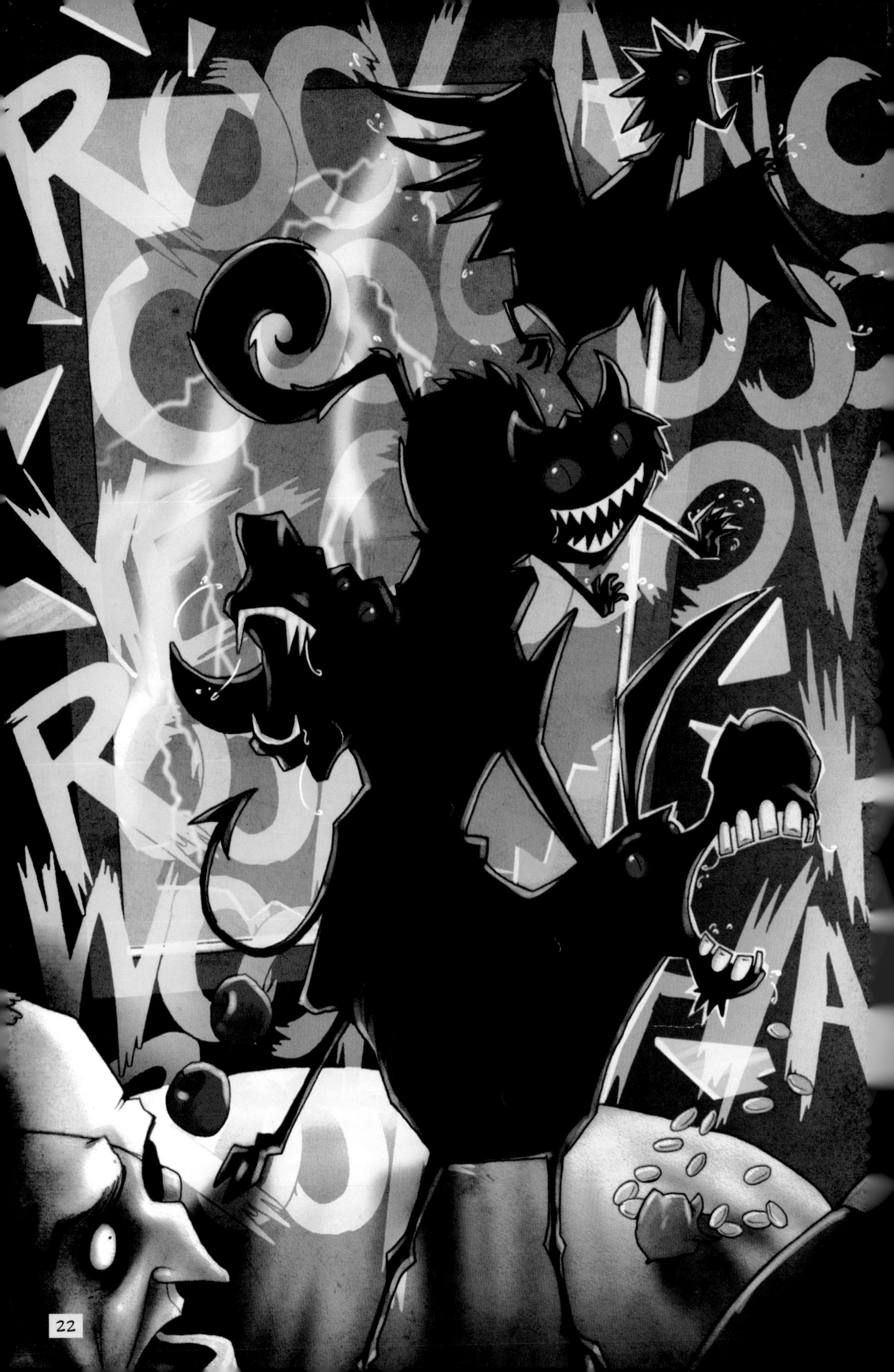

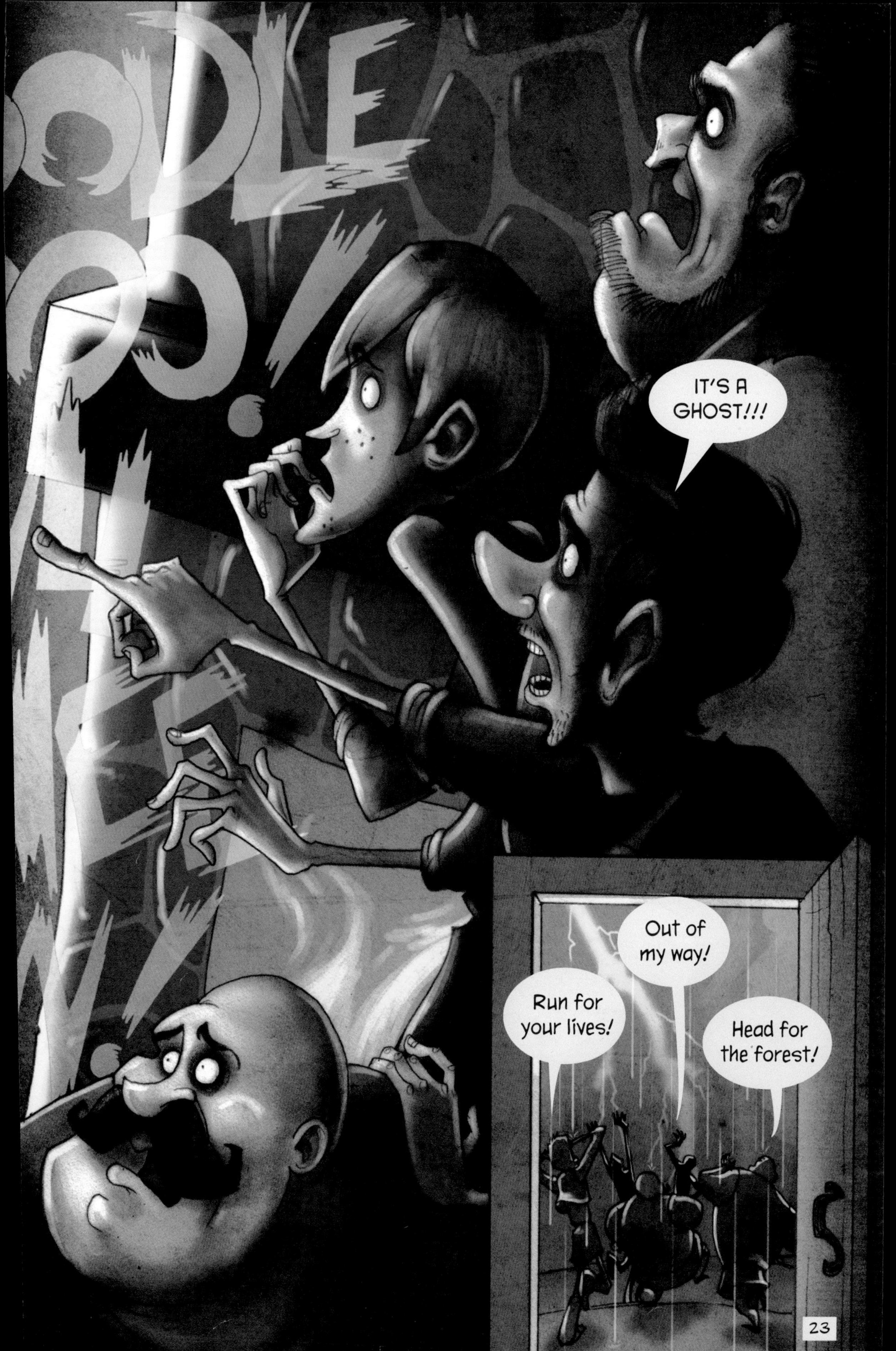
IT'S A GHOST!!!
Out of my way!
Run for your lives!
Head for the forest!

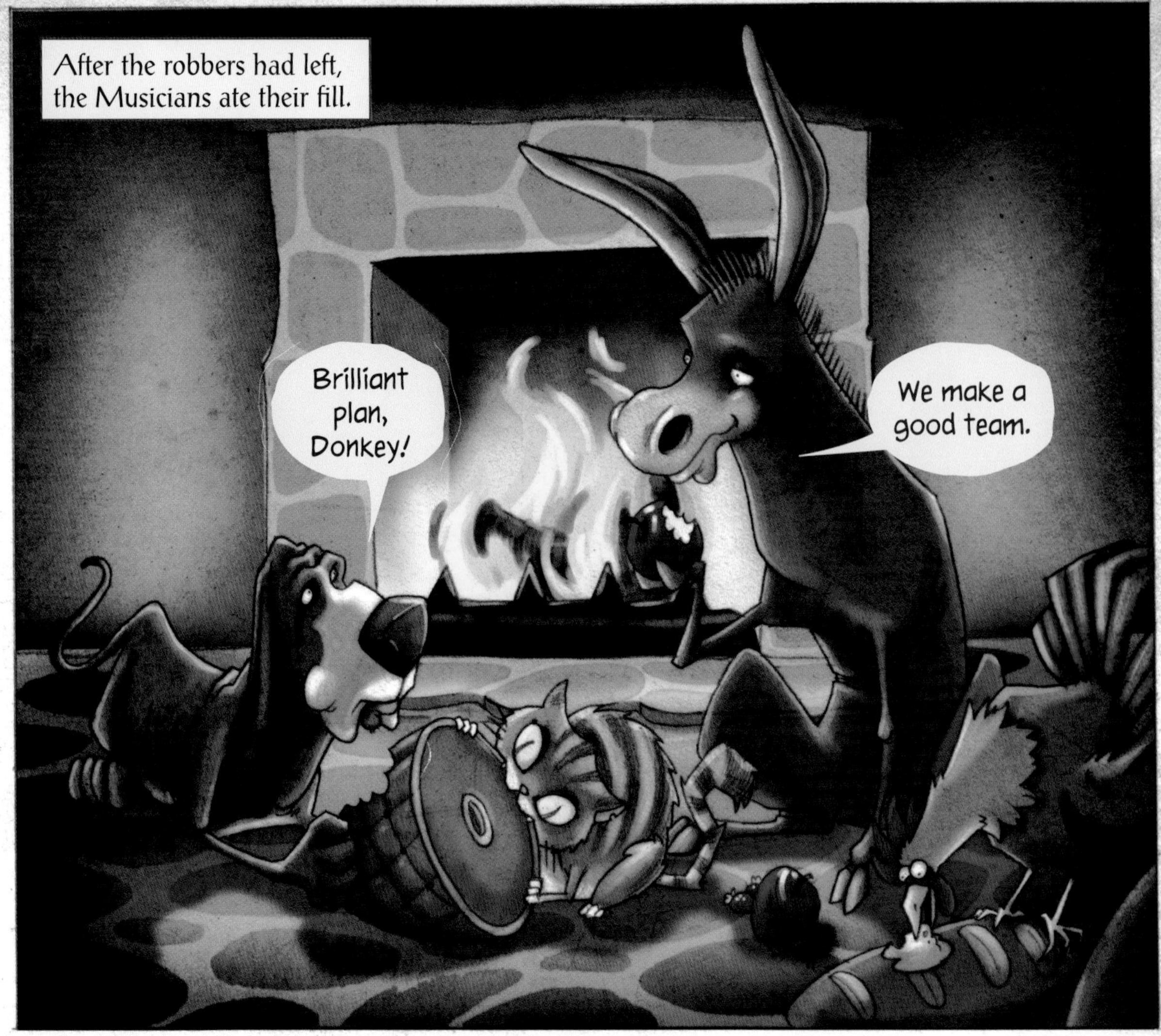
After the robbers had left, the Musicians ate their fill.
Brilliant plan, Donkey!
We make a good team.

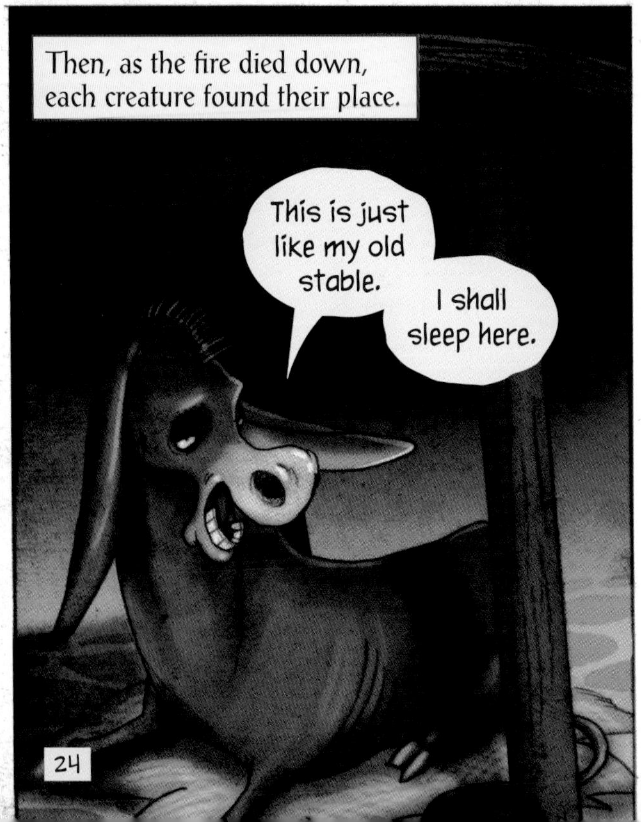
Then, as the fire died down, each creature found their place.
This is just like my old stable.
I shall sleep here.

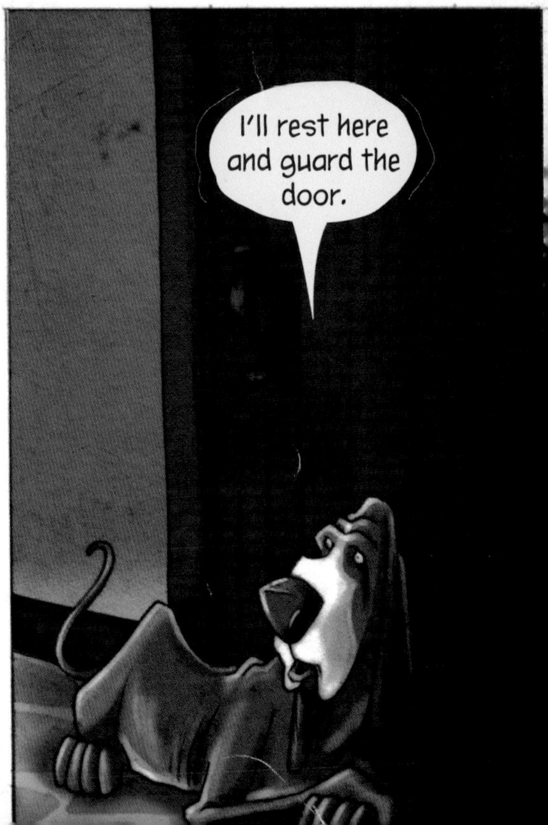
I'll rest here and guard the door.

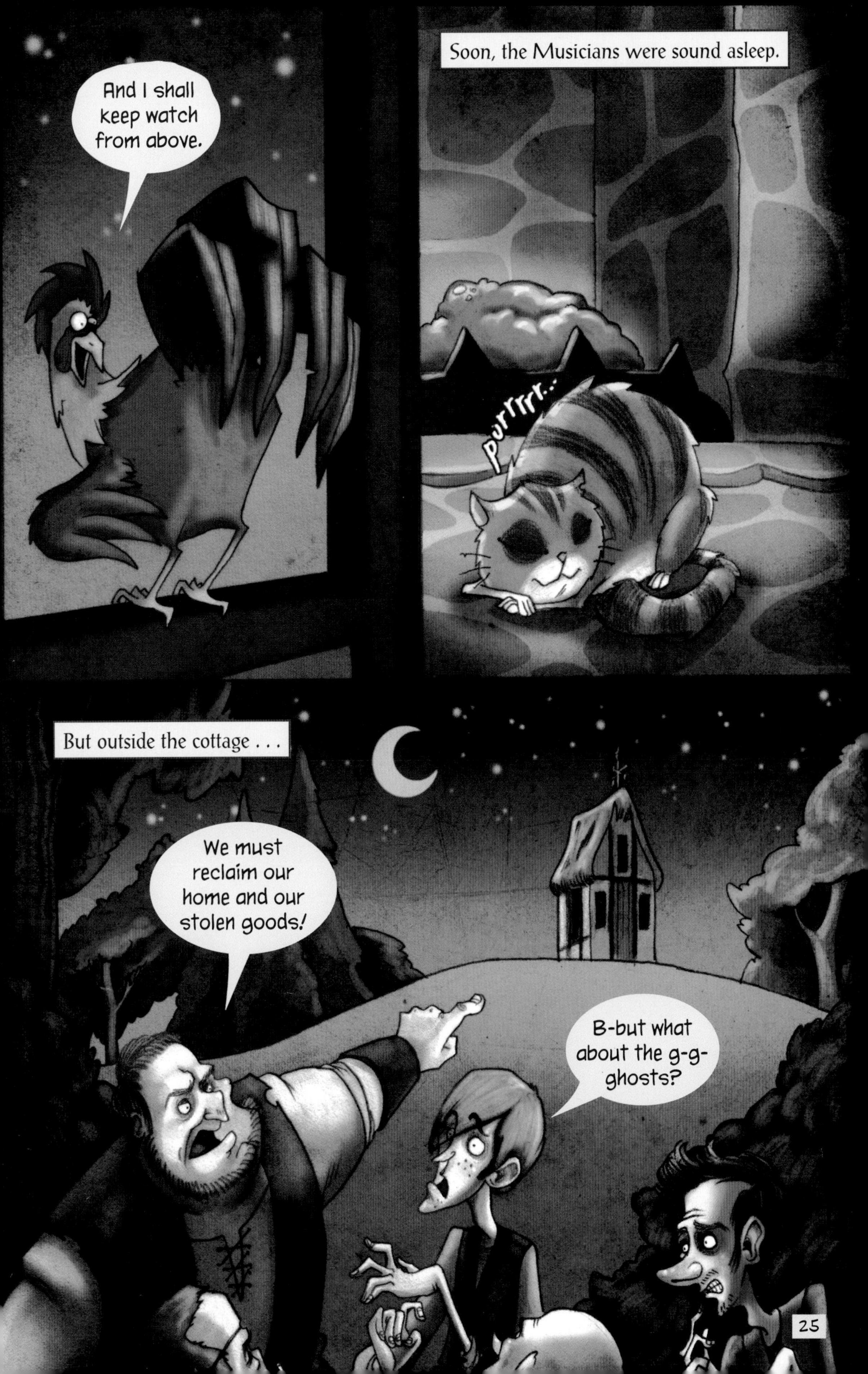
And I shall keep watch from above.
Soon, the Musicians were sound asleep.
purrrr...
But outside the cottage . . .
We must reclaim our home and our stolen goods!
B-but what about the g-g-ghosts?

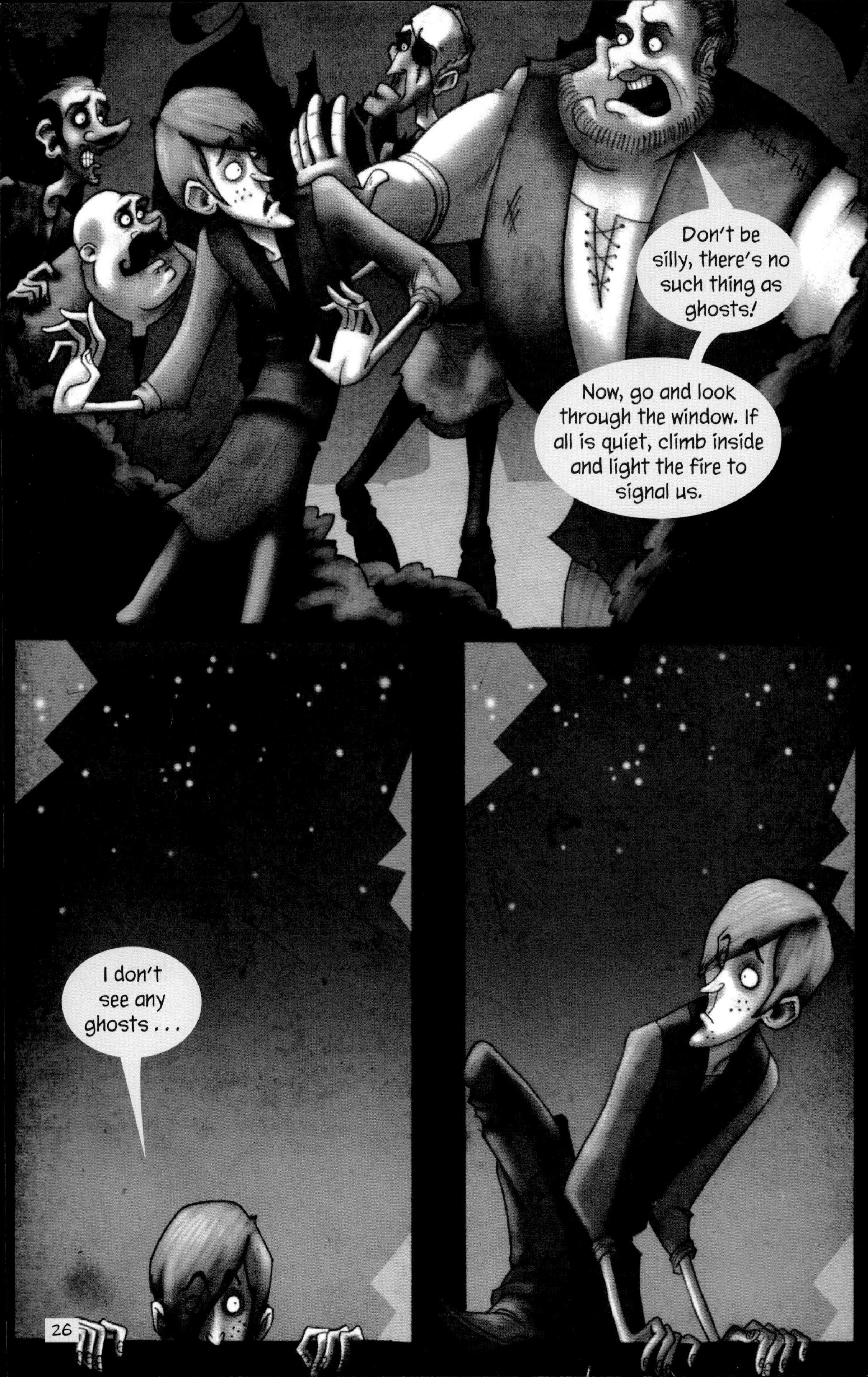
Don't be silly, there's no such thing as ghosts!
Now, go and look through the window. If all is quiet, climb inside and light the fire to signal us.
I don't see any ghosts . . .

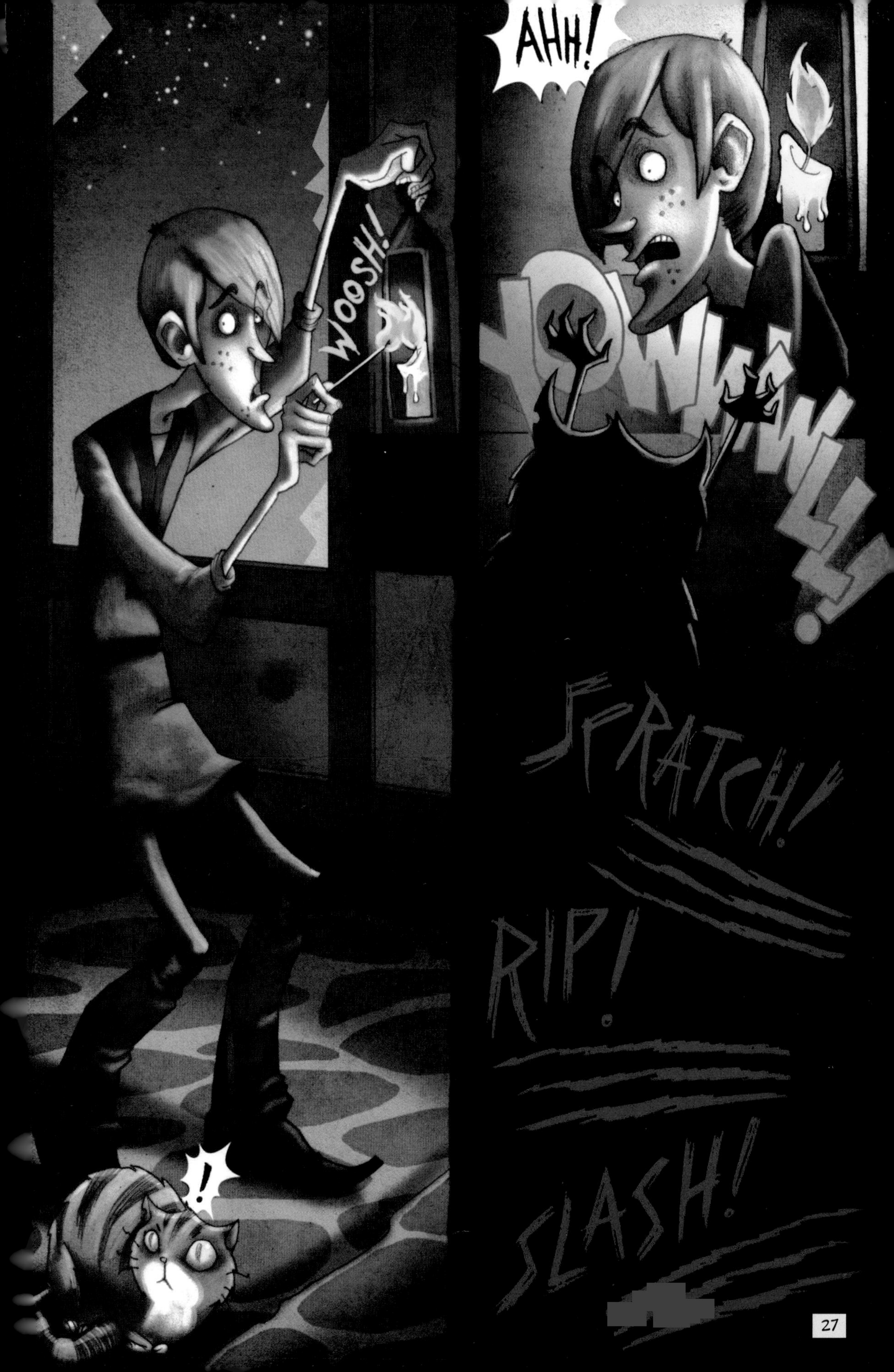
WOOSH!
!
AHH!
YOWWWLL!
SCRATCH!
RIP!
SLASH!

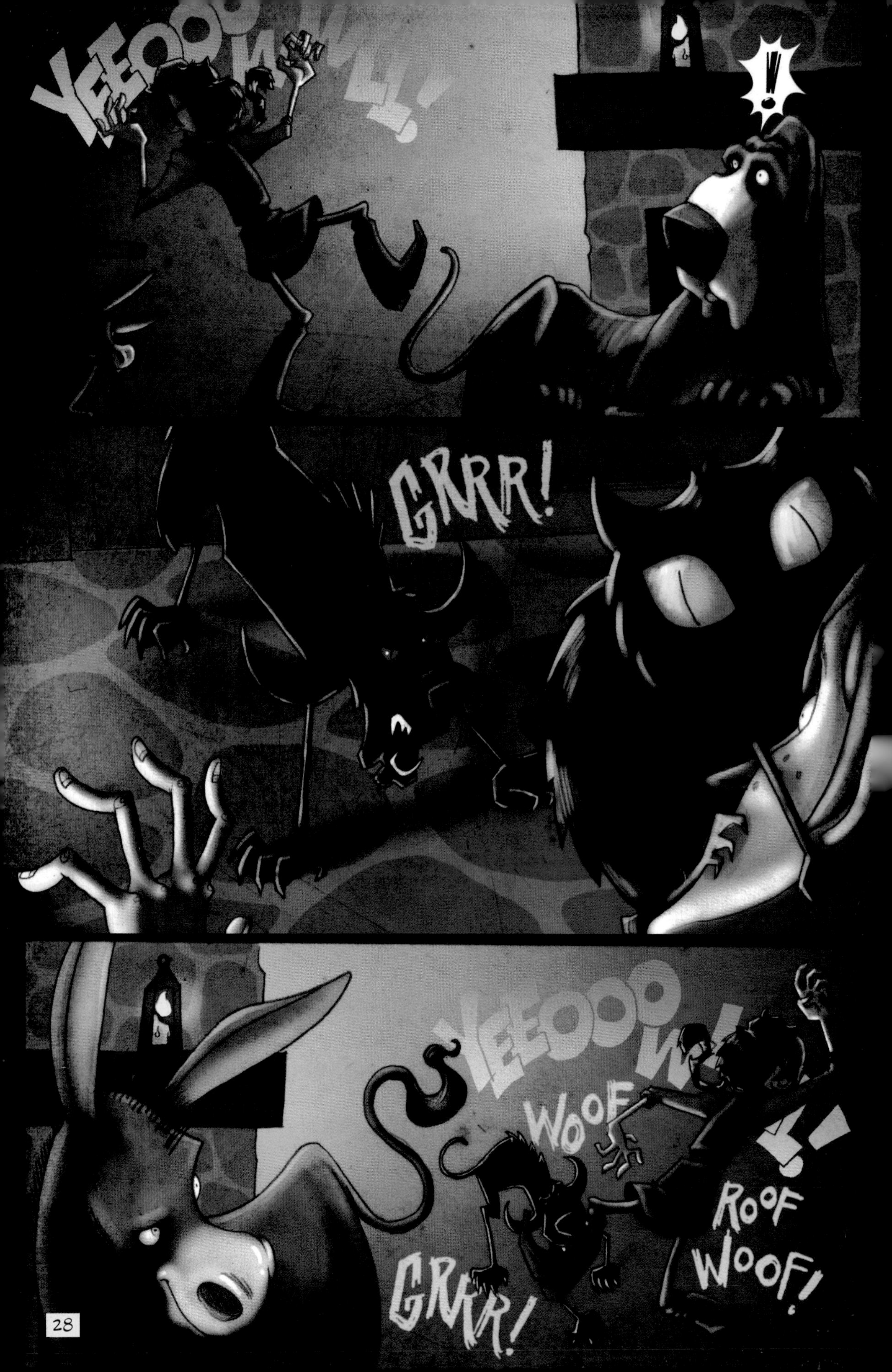
YEEOOWLL!
!
GRRR!
YEEOOOW!!
WOOF
ROOF
WOOF!
GRRR!

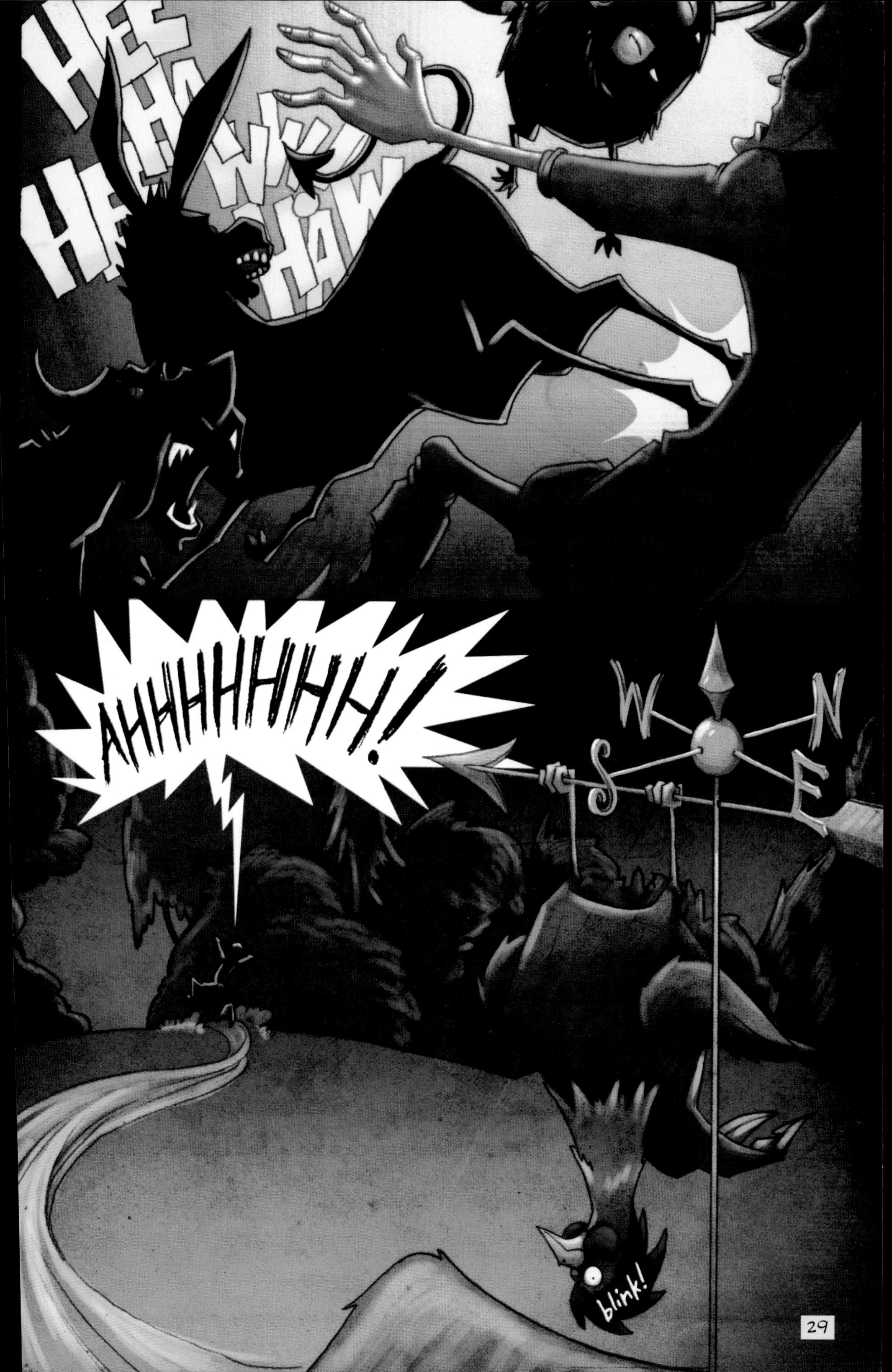
HEE
HAW
AHHHHHHH!
W
N
S
E
blink!

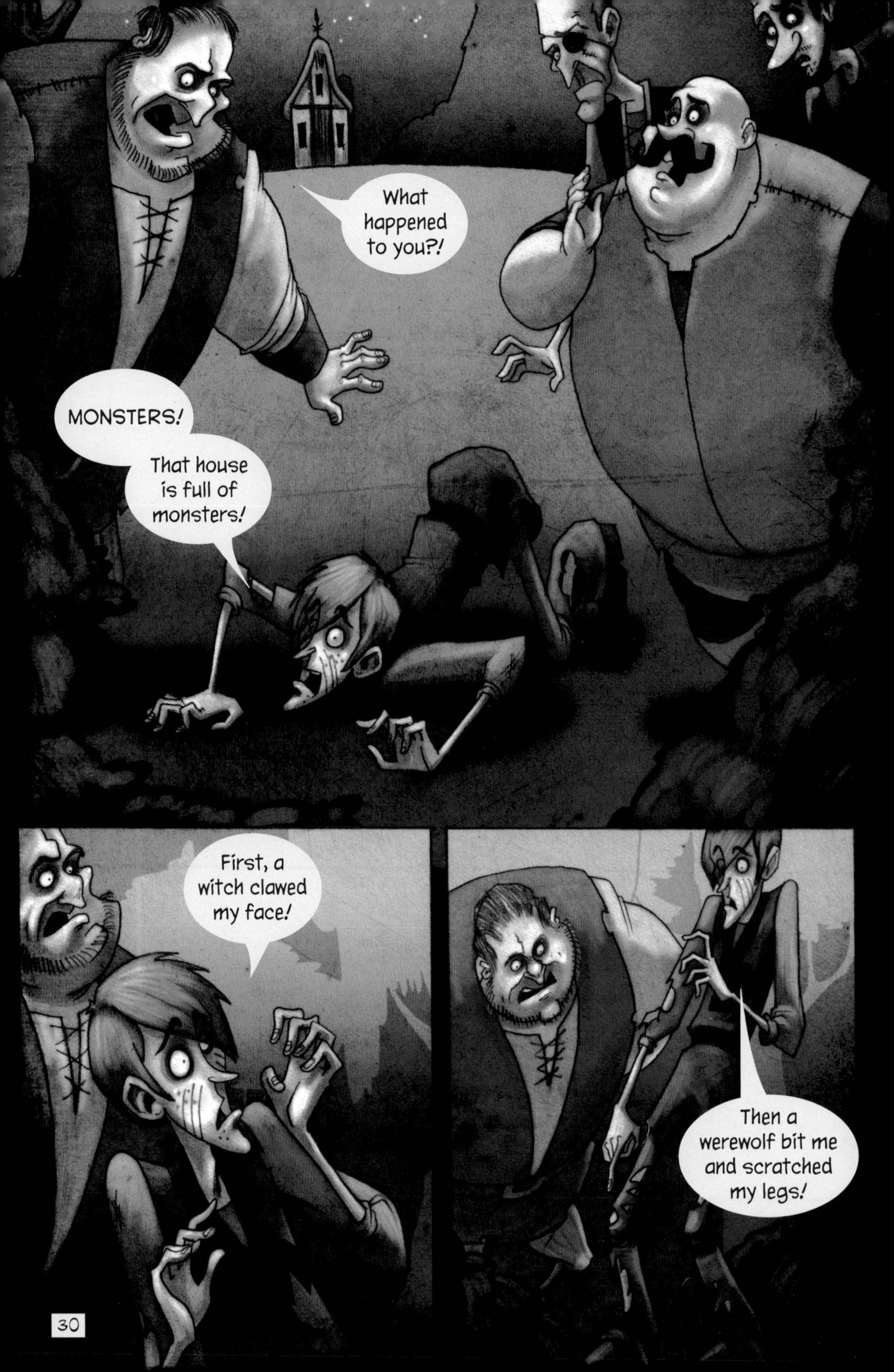
What happened to you?!
MONSTERS!
That house is full of monsters!
First, a witch clawed my face!
Then a werewolf bit me and scratched my legs!

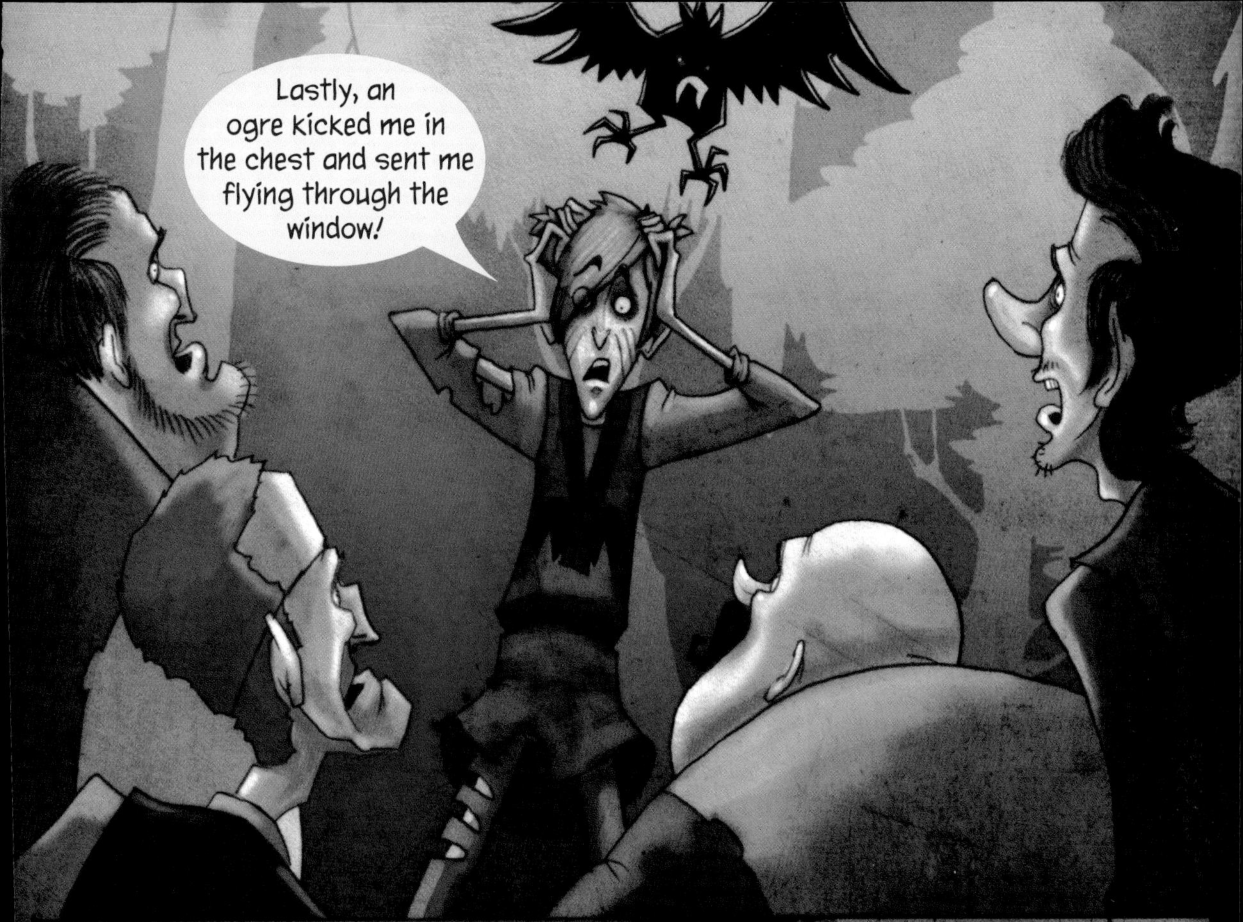
Lastly, an ogre kicked me in the chest and sent me flying through the window!

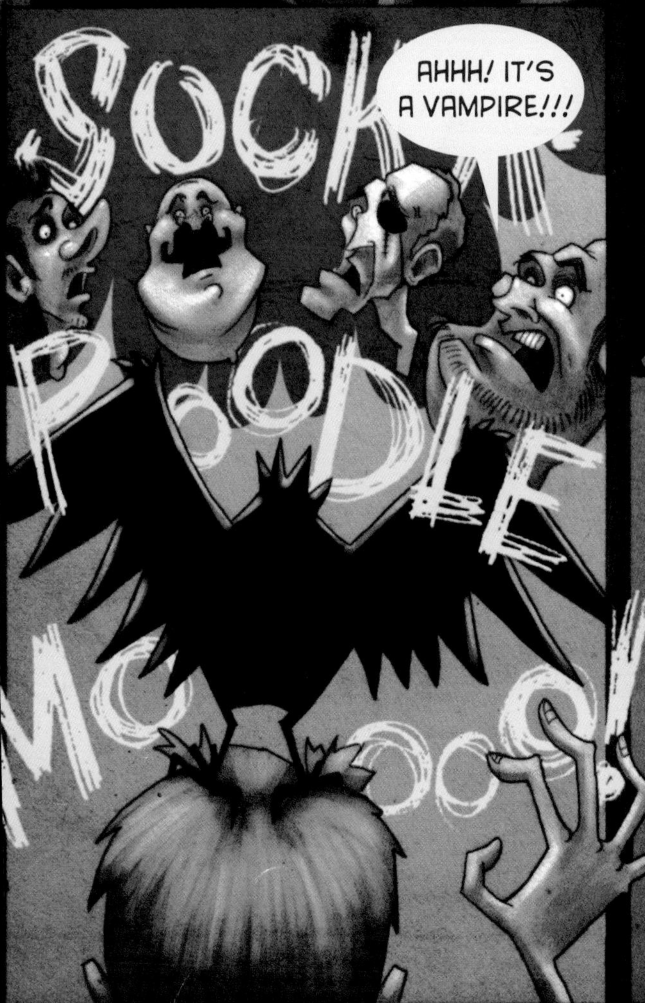
SOCK
AHHH! IT'S A VAMPIRE!!!
POODLE
MOOOOO!

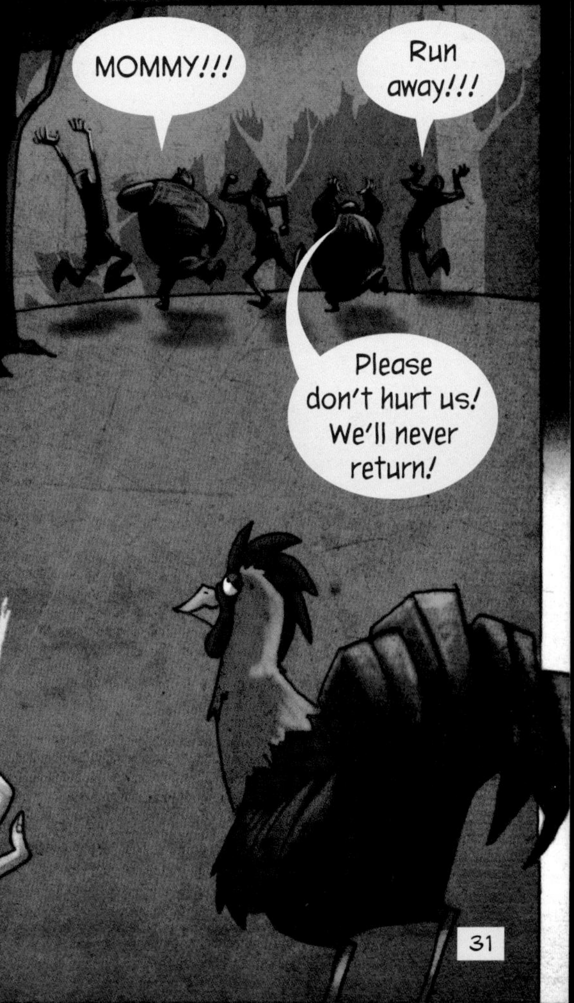
MOMMY!!!
Run away!!!
Please don't hurt us! We'll never return!

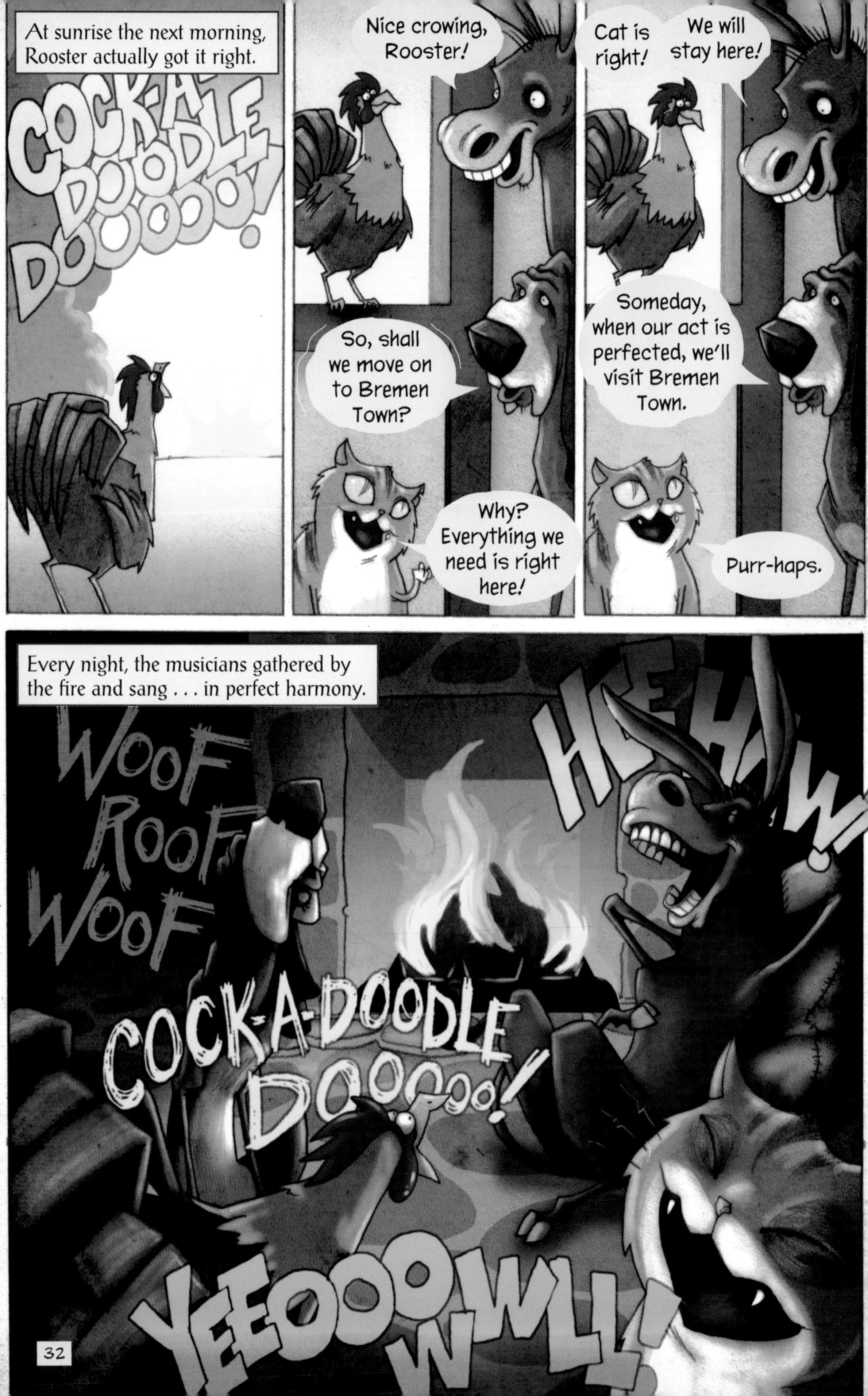
At sunrise the next morning, Rooster actually got it right.
COCK-A-DOODLE DOOOOOO!
Nice crowing, Rooster!
So, shall we move on to Bremen Town?
Why? Everything we need is right here!
Cat is right!
We will stay here!
Someday, when our act is perfected, we'll visit Bremen Town.
Purr-haps.
Every night, the musicians gathered by the fire and sang . . . in perfect harmony.
WOOF ROOF WOOF
HEE HAW!
COCK-A-DOODLE DOOOoo!
YEEOOOWWLL!

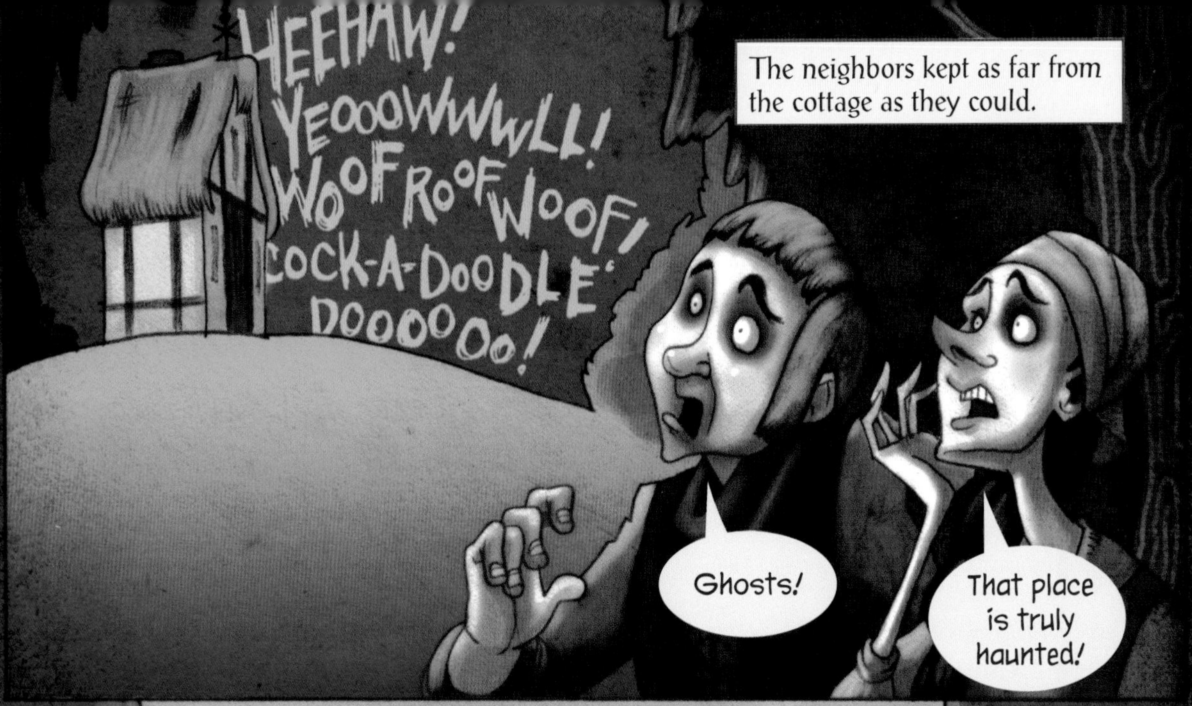
The neighbors kept as far from the cottage as they could.
HEEHAW!
YEOOOWWWLL!
WOOF ROOF WOOF!
COCK-A-DOODLE DOOOOOOO!
Ghosts!
That place is truly haunted!

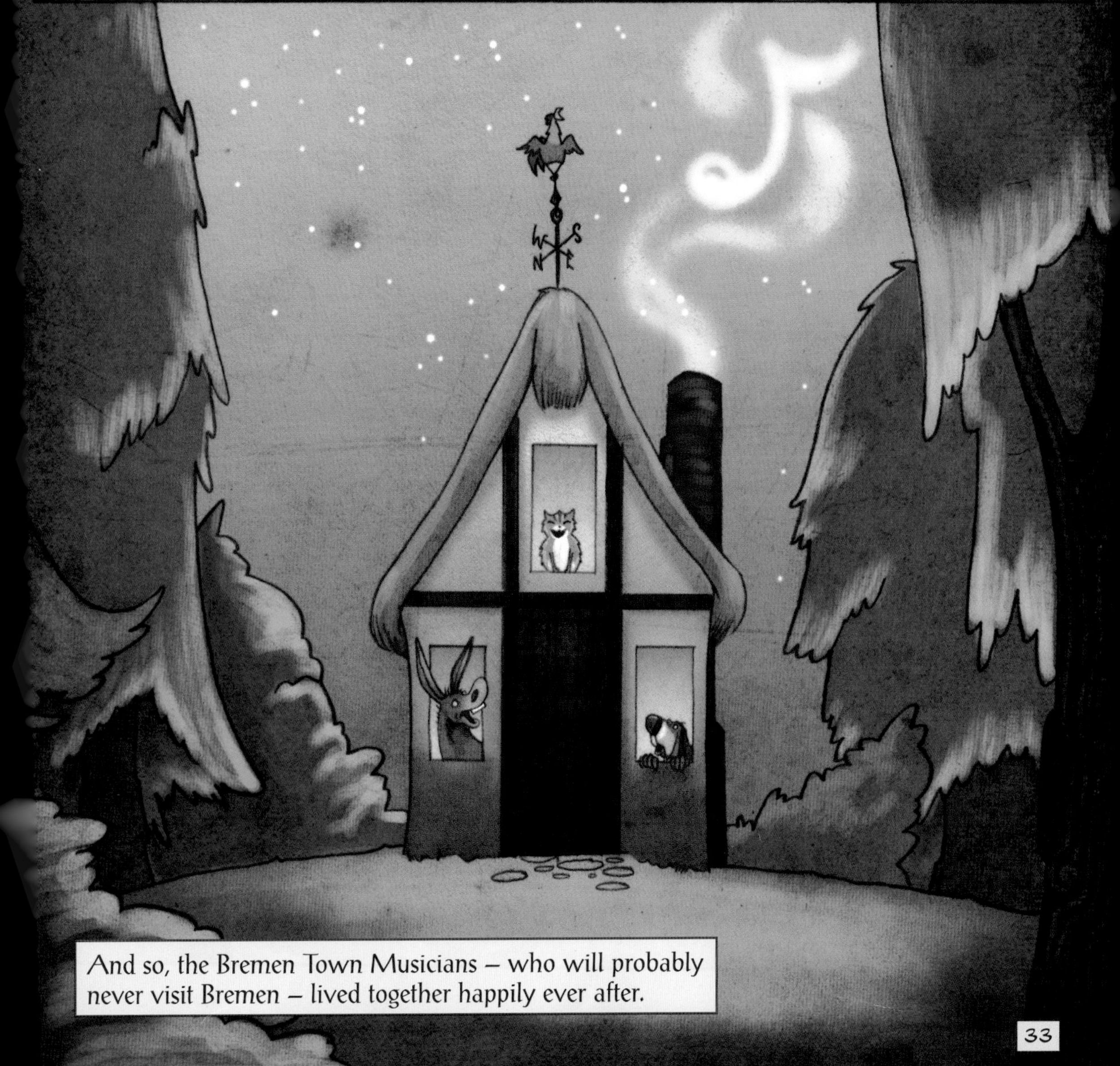
And so, the Bremen Town Musicians – who will probably never visit Bremen – lived together happily ever after.

THE BROTHERS GRIMM

A FAMILY OF FOLK AND FAIRY TALES

Jacob and Wilhelm Grimm were German brothers who invited storytellers to their home so they could write down their tales.

Peasants and villagers, middle-class citizens, wealthy aristocrats — even the Grimms' servants — contributed to their diverse collection of stories!

The brothers also collected folk tales from published works from other cultures and languages, adding to the variety of their sources.

In 1812, the Grimms published their collection of fairy tales, called *Children's and Household Tales.* The Brothers Grimm were among the first to collect and publish folk and fairy tales taken directly from the people who told them. These days, it would be hard to find anyone who hasn't at least heard of one of the Grimm Brothers' colorful characters!

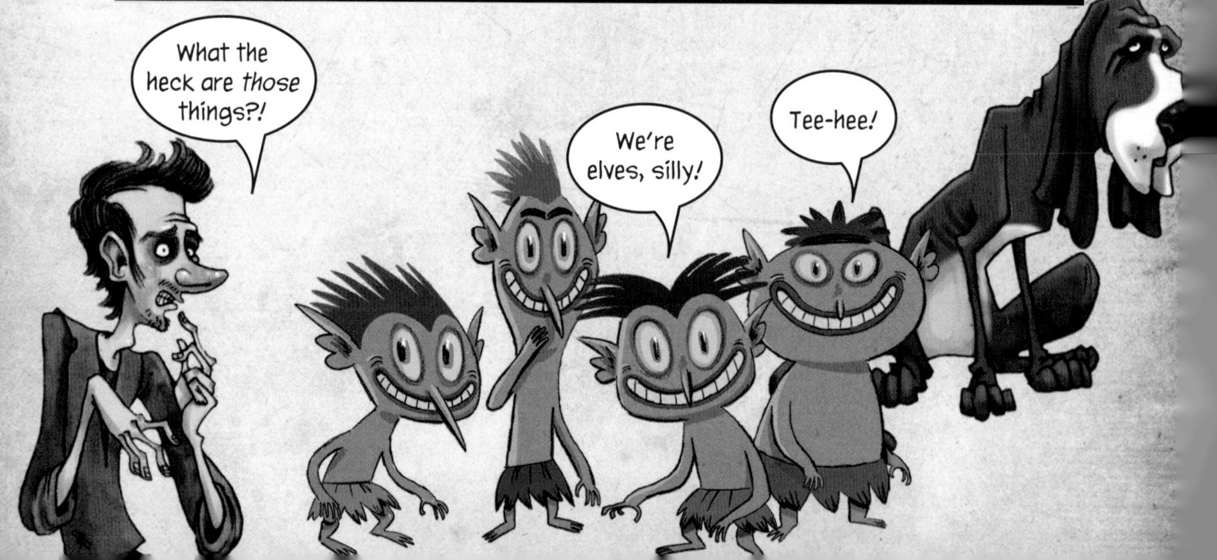
What the heck are *those* things?!
We're elves, silly!
Tee-hee!

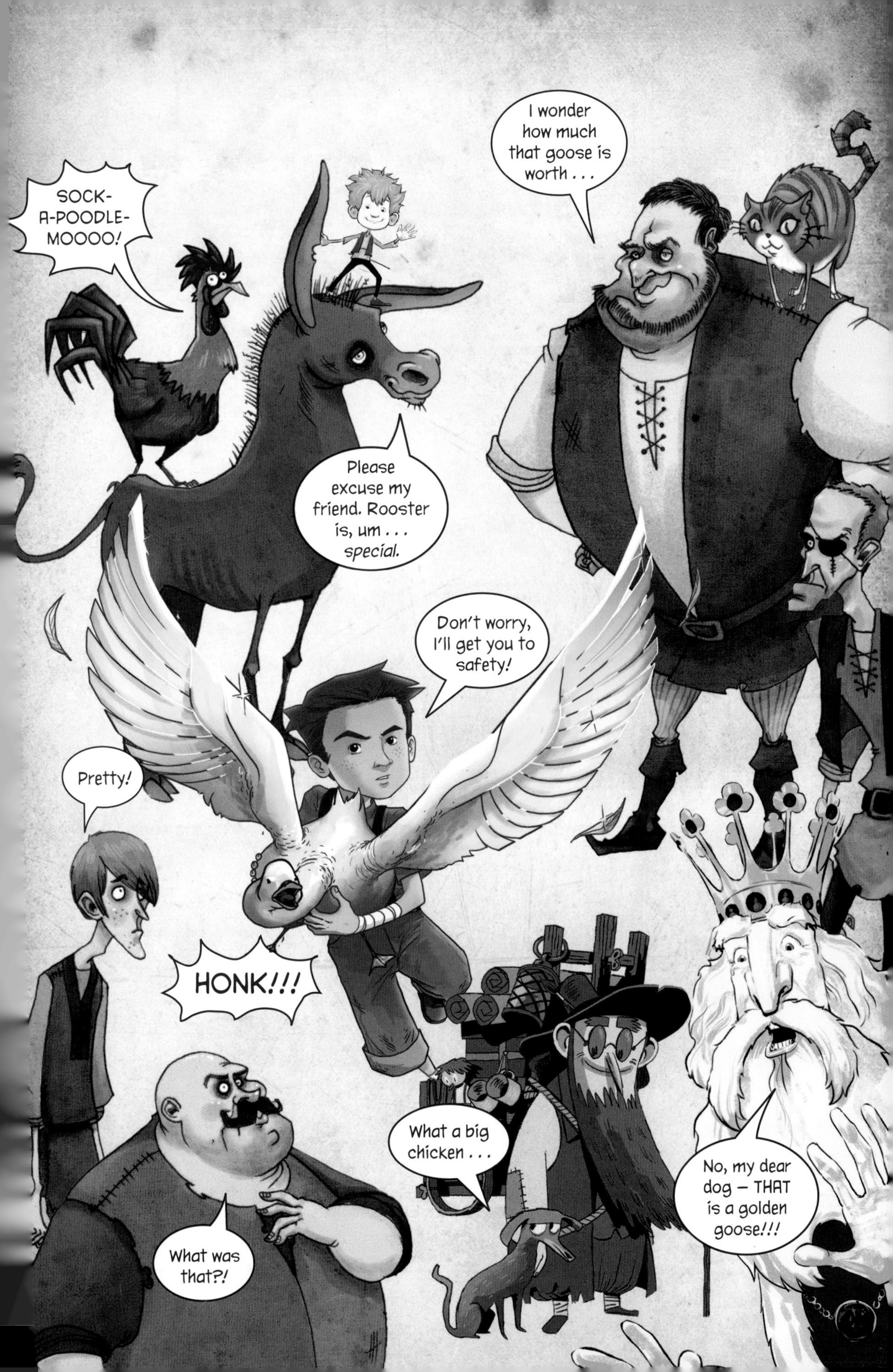
SOCK-A-POODLE-MOOOO!
Please excuse my friend. Rooster is, um . . . *special.*
I wonder how much that goose is worth . . .
Don't worry, I'll get you to safety!
Pretty!
HONK!!!
What a big chicken . . .
No, my dear dog — THAT is a golden goose!!!
What was that?!

Grab The Golden Goose

ABOUT THE RETELLING AUTHOR

Louise Simonson writes about monsters, science fiction and fantasy characters, and superheroes. She wrote the award-winning Power Pack series, several best-selling X-Men titles, Web of Spider-man for Marvel Comics, and Superman: Man of Steel and Steel for DC Comics. She has also written many books for children. She is married to comic artist and writer Walter Simonson and lives in the suburbs of New York City.

ABOUT THE ILLUSTRATOR

Lisa K. Weber is an artist who lives and works in Oakland, California. Her whimsically quirky characters and illustrations have appeared in various print and animation projects for Scholastic, Graphic Classics, Children's Television Workshop, and many others.

DISCUSSION QUESTIONS

1. The Bremen Town Musicians believe they have beautiful singing voices. Do you think the other characters in the story would agree with them? Why or why not?

2. Which one of the Bremen Town Musicians is your favorite character? Why?

3. Do you think the musicians will ever visit Bremen Town? Discuss your opinions.

WRITING PROMPTS

1. Imagine that a fifth animal has joined the other four Bremen beasts. What kind of animal is it? What sort of personality does it have? Write about your musical creature. Then, draw a picture of it.

2. Which illustration in this graphic novel is your favorite? What do you like about it? Re-draw the illustration in your own art style.

3. Imagine that the animal musicians finally head for Bremen Town. What new adventures do they have? What kinds of songs do they sing? Write about their journey.

GLOSSARY

BEAST (BEEST)—a wild animal

BRAY (BRAY)—when a donkey brays, it makes a loud, harsh noise

CREATURE (KREE-chur)—a living being, human or animal

ELEGANT (EL-uh-guhnt)—graceful and elegant, as in stylish

FRIGHTENING (FRITE-uhn-ing)—scary

HARMONY (HAR-muh-nee)—music that is played, or sung, at the same time and in the same chord

HAUNTED (HAWNT-id)—if a place is haunted, ghosts or evil spirits live there

HIDE (HIDE)—an animal's skin that is used to make leather

OGRE (OH-gur)—a fierce and cruel giant or monster

STARTLED (STAR-tuhld)—surprised or frightened someone and made them jump

TRUMPETS (TRUHM-pits)—announces the arrival of someone or something

More

GRIMM BROTHERS GRAPHIC NOVELS

by STONE ARCH BOOKS . . .

A GRIMM GRAPHIC NOVEL
THE ELVES and the SHOEMAKER

A GRIMM GRAPHIC NOVEL
The Golden Goose
retold by Sean Tulien
illustrated by Thiago Ferras

A GRIMM GRAPHIC NOVEL
TOM THUMB

Still want more?

Find cool websites and more books like this one at www.Facthound.com.

Just type in the Book ID: **9781434225184** and you're ready to go!

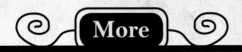

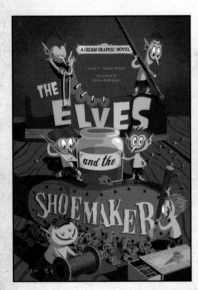

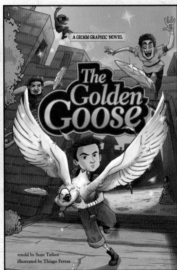

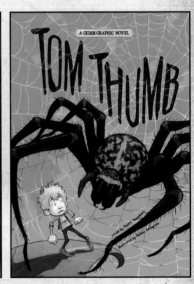